CROSSROADS
A TEENAGE SOLDIER IN WORLD WAR II

CHARLES SAMUEL BETTS

AuthorHouse™
1663 Liberty Drive
Bloomington, IN 47403
www.authorhouse.com
Phone: 1-800-839-8640

© 2010 Charles Samuel Betts. All rights reserved.

No part of this book may be reproduced, stored in a retrieval system, or transmitted by any means without the written permission of the author.

First published by AuthorHouse 9/16/2010

ISBN: 978-1-4520-6759-9 (hc)
ISBN: 978-1-4520-6760-5 (sc)
ISBN: 978-1-4520-6761-2 (e)

Library of Congress Control Number: 2010912573

Printed in the United States of America

This book is printed on acid-free paper.

Because of the dynamic nature of the Internet, any Web addresses or links contained in this book may have changed since publication and may no longer be valid. The views expressed in this work are solely those of the author and do not necessarily reflect the views of the publisher, and the publisher hereby disclaims any responsibility for them.

To Mary

In a man's life he needs two wives.
one as a companion and one as a mother of his children.
I was fortunate to have both in one wife
MARY

PROLOGUE

This is a story of a nineteen year old soldier in World War II. In the beginning, he was a frightened and confused teenager. His being thrust into battle and his meeting a beautiful young lady led to his metamorphosis into a mature fighting soldier. His experiences post war and the Korean War stabilized him and his wife and this led to many exciting years.

CHAPTER 1

It was a cold winter day, and Charles Bettendorf was all alone. He was just nineteen, and now, he was about to be sent overseas. How did he get to this point in his life? He tried to ponder this. Flashing memories came to his mind. He was seeing himself going to his mail box and getting an official letter. It said, "The United States Government". He hastily opened it fearing what it was. It was a draft notice. His name was on it. He was to report to Camp Robinson, Little Rock, Arkansas. The physical, the acceptance, the train trip to Camp Stewart, Georgia, all followed. He could go no further. His mind was distracted by thoughts of what he was facing. He couldn't focus his thinking. His thoughts seemed to scatter driven by his fear. He had been trained as an infantryman, and now, he was being sent to the Pacific to fight the Japs. All during his training, he had heard how brutal the Jap soldier was. His ability to fight in the jungle was frightening. Suddenly, there was a loud shout and a slamming of the door. A Sergeant was calling out names and announcing the following men were to report to a barge for loading. Bettendorf was the first name called. He was at Camp Stoneman, California, which was at the upper beaches of San Francisco Bay. It was about three p.m. and it would take three hours to get to the boat docks in San Francisco. Bettendorf had not heard a word from the Sergeant after his name had been called. He felt numb. He got slowly to his feet and turned in a daze to pack his duffle bag. It was hard to lift his arms, and he struggled. The Sergeant was shouting orders and demanding the men to hurry. He stumbled out of the barracks and slowly formed up into the squad, that was to be marched to the barge. He was numb, and he was on automatic. All he could do was put one foot in front of the other and follow the man in front of him.

His mind started working, and he found himself sitting on his duffle bag. He was looking around. The barge was being pushed by a tug boat. It was moving slowly. The bay was calm, and he could hear the lapping of the water as the barge was pushed slowly forward. As it progressed, the sun slowly sank in the west. It was getting dark when the barge was pushed to the pier where the troopship was moored. There were only black out lights that lit up the pier. The men were ordered onto the pier and told to lay down their duffle bags. Charles sat wearily on his bag and began to feel lost. It was the pain of the loss of the familiar. He was leaving the United States for how long? This question rolled back and forth in his mind. There was no answer. As he looked around, he could see the outlines of buildings. Out in the bay he could make out the outline of an island. He wondered, "What is its name?" In the midst of this revelry, he heard a harsh barking command. He was told his ship was on the other side of a big warehouse. This ship was a Dutch freighter converted into a troopship. Its name was the "Flying Dutchman". There was something foreboding about this ship. The approaching fog enveloped the ship and gave it a ghostlike appearance. He wondered if this ship was to be his grave. When he reached the other side of the pier, he immediately went up the gang plank. He was told to go down into the cargo hole of the ship and find his bunk. There was a stuffy odor in this cargo area, so here he was to bunk for 50 nights.

As he searched for a bunk, he became aware of the structure of this previous cargo hole. There were tiers of bunks stacked in fours. The top bunk allowed only 18 inches before it reached the ceiling. These bunks were off to the left of the stair case. They extended the length of the cargo hole. To the right were the latrine and the showers. There was no privacy.

He tested the water in the latrine and found that it was salt water. He put his duffle bag on the nearest bunk. He had no inclination to sleep there. He left and went to the top deck. There was a cool breeze blowing, and he felt refreshed. As he stood by the rail of the ship, he saw and heard much activity on the pier below. Men were lifting the ropes and chains that held the ship fast to the pier. There was much shouting of orders, and he heard the starting of the engines. The boat started moving forward and rubbed against the side of the pier. When it cleared the pier, a tug boat appeared and began maneuvering the boat into the main shipping channel of the bay. At this point, he became aware that the pilot had come aboard. The tug boat pulled away, and the ship picked up speed. He could feel the power of the ship and the confidence of the pilot. As the speed increased, he passed the island (Alcatraz). All of the buildings lining the shore were dark. He looked forward and could see the dim outline of a huge bridge. It was the Golden Gate Bridge. It seemed the ship moved all too rapidly as it approached the bridge. He knew that the Pacific Ocean lay beyond this bridge. Quickly he looked up and saw the ship was exactly under the bridge. There were some cars going over the bridge. He wondered if they had black out lights. As the bridge receded, he saw an empty black space. He looked down at the water and realized that the ship had entered an ocean of large swells. The Flying Dutchman had started to roll and pitch. At first, this didn't bother him as he was too involved with his feelings connected with his leaving his home and his country. He was thinking of Camp Stewart. It was a camp in a remote part of Georgia, near Hinesville, Georgia. At first, he was supposed to be trained in anti-aircraft artillery. As the need for this decreased, the training became basic infantry training. His thoughts were interrupted by the swells six to eight feet high. Soon he was retching and vomiting over the rail. He was not alone as many of his comrades were in the same condition. This seasickness was to last throughout the night and into the next day. During this time, he began to ask himself, why had he not developed any buddies. He felt all alone. He had been in the Army since May, and here it was mid-November.

As he explored this, memories came into focus. His first memory was of his experiences in grade school. He was two years ahead of his age in grade school. He had been advanced two grade levels as he had performed higher than his grade level. His classmates felt he was too young for them. His mind had matured, but his body had not. To make it worse, he was not athletically endowed. He tried to compete but was not successful. He had wanted to develop friends, but the only people interested in him were the ones that had the same problems. He reacted to this by being as smart as he could be. This was a very lonely solution. His mother had come from a wealthy family and constantly reminded him that he was better than most people because of his background. This gave him no comfort. All it did was encourage him to feel he was better than others when he really knew he was not. With this thought, he became aware that he was very hungry. It was then that he learned that food was only served two times a day. Breakfast started at 6:30 a.m., and it took until 11:00 a.m. to feed the 1200 enlisted men. The second meal started at 2:00 p.m. and lasted to 7:00 p.m. He looked at his watch and saw that it was 6:30 p.m. He rushed to the chow line and was among the last to be fed.

When he returned to the main deck, he saw the last rim of the sun sink below the waves. The surface of the sea darkened and the blackness of the night descended on him. There was no land in sight, and the darkness was oppressive. It was almost 48 hours since he had left San Francisco Bay. He had been told that the ship made eight knots an hour. He figured that he was about three hundred eighty-six miles at sea.

He decided that he would try to sleep on his bunk in the hole. He felt filthy from the residues of his seasickness and decided to take a shower. The shower area was empty, and he proceeded to shower. When he finished, he tried to dry off. It was impossible to get the layer of salt off his skin. He was very uncomfortable and slept poorly throughout the night. He decided to never bathe in salt water again and to sleep on the deck.

All enlisted men on this ship were replacements. There were no organizations to which they belonged. The officers, who were quartered on the stern of the ship, were in the same boat. They assumed no authority over the enlisted men. There were no organized activities. Everyone took care of themselves. There was no buddying going on. Groups of men were playing cards, but usually the men wandered in their space and tried to escape from their boredom. This was the situation of Charles' life for the next two weeks.

He got his sea legs and he lost his nostalgia. It was the passing of the big island, Hawaii, when he had an awakening. It all started with his finding a small paperback book the Army had issued to soldiers that were going overseas. In this book was a chapter on how one could determine their position in the ocean as they went to their destination. Charles read the following, "Find Your Place in the Sun." The easiest time to determine one's position is when the astronomical bodies pass overhead or reach their highest elevation above the horizon. Solar noon was when the sun was highest in the sky. On a clear day, it was easy to determine the time of a solar noon. A measurement of the sun around the solar noon could be used to determine longitude and latitude. This information started Charles on his first productive effort on a voyage that was to last many days.

The first thing he did was to build an instrument to determine the solar noon. From this, he determined the latitude and the longitude. He wanted to check his efforts and found a crew member, who had access to the ship's navigator. When the crewman showed his findings to the ship's navigator, he was surprised at the accuracy. Here again, Charles' knowledge gained him a new position. Not only did it give him a new friend, but it also came to the attention of the officers on the stern of the ship. They requested that he give a lecture on this process. The lecture was well received, and the officers gave him permission to spend time with them on the stern of the ship. They wanted him to give further lectures, which he did for the rest of the voyage.

This experience brought to mind many experiences of the past. His first memory was of his first grade teacher. He was in a one room school house in Riverton, Louisiana, and he was with children from the first to the sixth grade. His teacher quickly became aware of Charles' quick ability to learn. She advanced him and was excited to have him as a student. She praised him, and he blossomed under her teaching. She was his first love. She was a pretty, petite, young lady. She had dark brown hair and dark blue eyes. She was Miss Fourshey. There were many other experiences of this type in grade school, high school, and college.

In grade school, he had his first experience of the difficulties in jumping a grade in school. He was too advanced in his knowledge to stay in the third grade. His teacher recommended him to be advanced to the fourth grade. This displeased his fourth grade teacher as she felt that she would have to do catch up work. She wanted to prove that he was not capable to be in her class. She focused on him with the idea that she could prove that he was not able to be in her class. She put far more pressure on him than her other students. She would assign more home work to him with the idea that he was behind the class. The more she would expect from him excited him. He felt that they were in a race trying to see who could win. Each of them was determined to win. He was for knowledge, and she was for proving he didn't deserve to be in her class. As it progressed, she began to realize that she was really giving more of her teaching time to him than the other students. He was becoming her main student. She also realized that he was becoming more advanced in her class. If she continued, he would be eligible to go to the next grade level. One day she asked him to stay after class. It was about 4:00 p.m. and everything in the building was very quiet. All of the noises of children were gone. He was uneasy as he knew that she didn't want him in her class. He expected that she was going to tell him he was not able to keep up with the class. He was prepared to say he was. She started off by saying she guessed that he knew by now she did not think he was ready for the fourth grade. She had pushed him, so as to prove this idea was true. He had really amazed her. He had accepted her challenges and asked for more. He had become the student that all teachers longed for. He was a student, who wanted to absorb as much knowledge as that teacher could present. She realized now she had created a student that was approaching mid-term at the level that existed in the fifth grade. She did not want to advance him. She wanted to keep him in her class. From now on, he would receive only regular fourth grade instruction. If he wanted more studies, she would give him a reading list that she thought would interest him. He thanked her for accepting him in her class, and he would like her list. The rest of the year was very different. She enjoyed him, and he enjoyed her. She alerted his fifth grade teacher that he was a sponge, that soaked up all of her teachings and asked for more.

These memories were troubling to him. Were they the reason why he never had any friends? Was he so preoccupied with learning that he had had no desire for friends? He went through his next two grades much the same. In the seventh grade, he had his first male teacher. There were some rowdy boys in that class. They were always in trouble. He wanted to be a part of that group and tried to be rowdy, also. This ended in him and this group being held after school. They were paddled. This convinced him that this was not the way to go. It wasn't that he was not accepted by this group after this experience, it was that he just wanted to learn, and they didn't.

It was in the eighth grade that he met Mrs. B.D. Reeves. They quickly developed a warm teacher-student relationship. His family had a long time relationship with her husband. Her husband owned a department store in El Dorado, Arkansas, located on the square. In the center of El Dorado was located a large courthouse. There were streets surrounding this building. Businesses were located all around this square facing the courthouse. Mr. B.W. Reeves, not only supplied their clothing, but also financed his grandfather every year. Every year when his grandfather needed money to buy seed to plant his spring crop, he would mortgage his farm to Mr. Reeves. Mr. Reeves was a tall, gray-headed man and was quiet and gentle in his business dealings. Back to Mrs. Reeves -- she was interested in stimulating him in many different areas. She entered him in a musical identification contest. She spent hours educating him in recognizing famous operas and symphonies. He won the contest, and his name was in the newspaper. His high school years were the same. It was a math teacher in his freshman year, a world history teacher in his sophomore year and a French teacher and a chemistry teacher in his junior and senior years. How did this thinking come about? Oh, yes, he was wondering how all of this desire to excel came about. It was a mixture of wanting to know and the encouragement of important teachers in his life.

More important realities were coming into his awareness. How was he going to bathe? He had found that a salt water bath was so unpleasant. This turned out not to be a problem. After a few days, the ship was in tropical waters and rain showers were frequent. He simply would go out in the rain, soap up, and bathe himself. This worked fine until one day when he was about five degrees below the equator. He was bathing when all of a sudden a water spout formed and engulfed him. Why wasn't he sucked up in the water spout? He decided he was in the water shell of the spout and not in the suction part.

As the days passed, he established a pattern of behavior. He would lecture to the officers, do his solar noon, and meet with his crew friend. Each day he would report the ship's position. When they crossed the equator, an initiation was ordered for those, who had never crossed the equator (in his time overseas, he would cross the equator four times). This involved various punishments. The one Charles objected to was crawling through a line of people with paddles. The paddlers were too vicious for him, and he refused. He didn't get his shellback, which was the award for going through the initiation.

The nights around the equator were very interesting to him. He would see flying fish during the day, and some would land on the deck. At night he would watch the phosphorescence of the sea. The seas would light up from thousands of small organisms, who emitted light.

One day with his solar noon, he found that the ship would, if it continued on course, pass by San Christobal Island. At 3:00 p.m., the island was sighted. This island was very close to Guadalcanal and was in the Soloman group of islands. The next day Charles passed by the south shore of Guadalcanal. The north shore was the location of Henderson Field. The Japanese did land troops on the south shore, but the slot (the north shore) was where the big naval battles were fought. Since the ship Charles was on was unescorted, it traveled off the main shipping lanes in order to avoid Japanese submarines. It was two days later that the Flying Dutchman anchored at Finchhaven, New Guinea.

Three hundred seventeen miles due east of Finchhafen on the island of New Britain was a Japanese naval base called Rabaul. This base was bypassed by MacArthur. No one was allowed to disembark. The ship stayed in the harbor for several days.

CHAPTER 2

A big battle was being fought at Aitapi south of Hollandia, New Guinea. With this news, the ship immediately lifted anchor, and the ship sped to Hollandia. This was the first time he realized how big New Guinea was. It was about 700 miles from Finchhaven to Hollandia. The ship arrived about 8:00 a.m. and anchored. Charles expected to be taken off ship as it was reported infantry replacements were needed. The ship stayed for one week. Hollandia had a small harbor. On the north side was a tall hill. On top of this hill was a white house. He was told that this was the headquarters of General MacArthur. They said, "His family lived there." The need for troops abated, and the ship left for Leyte. Leyte was over 1400 miles away, and Charles expected this was where he would enter combat. He started reading in earnest infantry tactics and stopped doing navigation.

The ship passed close to many islands under Japanese control. The crewman friend, Eli Barnes, and he talked about their parting. They didn't know if they would ever see each other again as each would be in remote areas. Postal service would be irregular or nonexistent. They had become close friends. Many times, they had talked together about current activities but had never talked about their lives prior to the war. They decided to talk about their other lives.

Eli started by saying he came from a large family. He was raised in a small town in South Central Kansas, Salina. His father had a large farm, and their main crop was wheat. He had never liked farming and from an early age wanted to go to sea. He had applied to join the Navy and the Coast Guard and was turned down by both because of color blindness. He joined the Merchant Marines, in 1940. He was now in the process of trying to become an officer. For the last five years, he was satisfied to be an ordinary seaman. Now, he wanted to become an engineer. He knew that this service did not require that you be able to see colors. He was now 26 years old, and he was engaged to a childhood sweetheart. As soon as the ship unloaded its troops, they were supposed to load up some soldiers and go to Hawaii. From there, it was to San Diego. Eli planned to jump ship and go to Kansas to marry his fiancee'. Charles related his story. They felt that they had some way to connect up after the war. It was several months later he heard that the Flying Dutchman had been sunk, and all on board were lost at sea. Charles was very grateful to this friend because on many occasions, he would share his food with him.

The trip to Leyte was much more dangerous as the Japanese still held many islands that he would pass. All of the troops were aware of this danger. Charles was not anxious. He was becoming aware that he didn't seem to react to danger easily. He just went about his business and didn't consider the possible danger. After about a week, he arrived at Tacloban, Leyte. He had seen no land for 1,000 miles. He looked out to shore and saw palm trees and signs of a small village.

After a couple of days, a landing craft pulled up to the Flying Dutchman, and a net was dropped over the side of the ship. He was ordered to disembark. The night before, he had said goodbye to his crew friend. Both realized that they would probably never see each other again. Just before he was to get on the net, he heard a shout saying, "Charles". He looked around and spotted Eli. They both waved and shouted goodbye. Climbing down the rope net was difficult as he was carrying his duffle bag on his back. It was only one mile to shore and in a short time, he was on land for the first time in fifty days. A troop-carrying vehicle took him to the replacement camp (Repo Depo Camp). From this time onward, he would be in an active war zone.

He was immediately marched to a processing center. When they reviewed his record, they noted that he had been in college and had studied pre-med courses for two years. Since there was a shortage of medical personnel, he was temporarily assigned to the aid station. Because he had a major in biology, he was assigned to develop a demonstration of how schistosomiasis was transmitted. This meant that he would go to rice paddies and collect specimens of earlier stages of development of the worm parasite. These were the stages in the water of the rice paddies, that infected the troops. He was very careful while he collected these specimens as he knew how dangerous it was to be infected. He would give lectures on how the larva stage of this parasite would invade the skin and begin to circulate in the blood stream. The larva would mature, but they would have no way to escape. They would form aggregates of parasites and destroy the surrounding tissue.

CHAPTER 3

For the first few days, things went well. There were Red Cross personnel attached to the aid station, and he found himself attracted to a cute little blond headed gal, Lillian Kenworth. She paid no attention to him, and he knew his interest was going nowhere.

It was early one morning. He was waiting to go off night duty when in walked Lillian. No one else was in the station at that time. She had left some of her equipment and was beginning to collect it when there was a burst of machine gun fire. Charles looked out of the tent in the direction of the shots and saw Japanese soldiers advancing on the depot. The aid station was directly in their path of assault. The aid station kept a M-1 rifle with ammo, and he immediately grabbed it. He pulled the frightened Lillian into a sheltered position. He started firing back at the advancing Japs. He saw two Jap soldiers fall. The attacking Japanese were paratroopers, who had been dropped on the outskirts of the depo with a suicide mission of search and destroy. They had orders to avoid resistance and to destroy as long as they lived. Since Charles was putting up a strong resistance, they bypassed his position and continued their advance. Lillian clung to Charles and, at times, hindered his fire. She was terrified. He continued to fire on the Japanese as fast as he could. The whole action lasted about 45 minutes.

There was a combat unit camped adjacent to the replacement depot. They had been depleted in the ongoing battle for Ormoc in western Leyte. They were able to respond quickly and rapidly pushed the Japanese paratroopers away from the replacement depot. Eventually, they surrounded them at the Buie Air Field. It took awhile to destroy them.

Even with the firing being over, he still found Lillian clinging to him. Slowly, he was able to calm her down, and he led her to a bench. Just before the assault, he had made the morning coffee. He got her a cup of coffee. At this moment, an officer from the combat unit, that had repulsed the attack, came in. He had noted that there were many dead Japanese soldiers around the aid station. He wanted to know, who was in charge of defending the aid station. Before Charles could respond, Lillian shouted out, "He was," pointing to Charles. The officer could not believe that only one man could hold off such a determined attacking force. He said, "There are several dead Japanese soldiers around the aid station." He interviewed Charles and left. Shortly, the morning crew arrived, and Lillian excitedly related, what had happened. Things began to settle down, and Charles was relieved of his duties. Lillian couldn't let go of Charles. He was pleased with her need for him but felt that it was just a reaction to the intense danger they had just experienced. They walked over to a recreational area, and for the first time talked about themselves.

Lillian was from Athens, Georgia. She had been in college, and when she reached the age that she could work in the Red Cross, she joined up for foreign service. Her Father had been in the regular Army and was seriously wounded in the early days of the war. He received a medical discharge. Lillian wanted to be involved in the war, and this led to her joining the Red Cross.

Charles told about his coming from El Dorado, Arkansas. He related how he was at Vanderbilt University studying pre-med. In his second year of college, he was told that he would be drafted, and he was given the opportunity to volunteer which he did. The talk drifted to more casual subjects. Charles asked her if he could see her again. She replied with a big "yes". So, it seemed that maybe this was going to be a great romance, but other forces were at work.

The officer that had interviewed Charles reported back to his company commander. He reported about the skirmish around the aid station. Since his unit had been withdrawn from the front line because of severe casualties, they were searching for replacements. The company commander, Captain Sam Petrie, was interested in competent replacements. He asked First Lieutenant Joe Schmidt if he got the name and serial number of this private, who single handedly held off the attacking Japanese paratroopers. He said, "Joe, you know how hard it was for us to destroy that attacking force. We need men like this soldier." Joe recognized his mistake and immediately went back to the aid station. Sergeant Maloney, who was in charge of the station, was talking with his staff. He told them that they must act quickly and get Charles assigned to his staff on a permanent basis. At this point, Lieutenant Schmidt arrived. He asked for the name, rank, and serial number of the soldier, who had defended the aid station. Sergeant Maloney, with great reluctance said, "Private Charles Bettendorf, 38668541." Lieutenant Schmidt told Sergeant Maloney his unit wanted this man, and they were immediately requesting him as a replacement for Company A, 1st Battalion, 132nd Calvary Regiment, attached to the First Calvary Division. Sergeant Maloney knew that this unit had first claim on replacements. With a deep sigh, he gave up his desire to keep Private Bettendorf.

When Lillian's commander, Helen Hatfield, heard of her narrow escape, she immediately began to consider how much danger to which her staff was being exposed. She left her station and began trying to find Lillian. Lillian and Charles were in a remote area of the post exchange. This exchange was for enlisted men only, and the men, that were there wondered how a private, who was just a replacement could rate such a beautiful girl. A short time later, Commander Hatfield found Lillian with a soldier. This irritated her as her staff was not to date the soldiers. She blustered into their conversation and demanded, "What are you doing in this exchange talking to a soldier, and a private at that?" Lillian calmly rose and said, "Private Charles Bettendorf has saved my life, and I will be eternally grateful to him. If any time he wants to talk to me, I will be available." When Commander Hatfield realized who Private Bettendorf was, she apologized. She thanked him for saving Lillian's life. She said, "Under these circumstances, I whole heartily agree with Lillian." She gave Lillian the rest of the day off, and since Charles was off duty, they decided to get lost so that they could get better acquainted. It was a wonderful day for them, and it would sustain their relationship for the troubling times that were to come.

When Charles reported for his night shift duties, he was greeted by an angry Sergeant Maloney. He asked, "Where have you been? I have searched all over the camp for you. You have been assigned to Company A, 1st Battalion, 132nd Cavalry Regiment. You are to report immediately to Captain Petrie." Bettendorf asked where was he located. Maloney called Captain Petrie and was told a man would come to get Private Bettendorf. Bettendorf packed his duffle bag and left a message with Sergeant Maloney telling Lillian where he was locating. Private Bill Williams arrived at the aid station. He was angry about having to give up a poker hand to pick up a replacement. He couldn't understand why a replacement was receiving such special attention.

Captain Petrie knew as soon as the information got out about Private Bettendorf's defense of the aid station, he would be sought by many infantry units. A good replacement was hard to get. He felt the need to grab him as soon as possible. He had been frustrated all day trying to get him transferred and was relieved that he was found. As

Williams and Bettendorf walked to Captain Petrie's office, Williams complained bitterly about all the trouble Bettendorf was causing him. After all, he was just a replacement. When they arrived, Williams was surprised about how warmly Captain Petrie greeted Bettendorf. When Bettendorf arrived in front of Captain Petrie, he came to attention and saluted saying, "Private Charles Bettendorf reporting as ordered." Williams was dismissed, and Charles was told to stand at ease. Captain Petrie told Charles he was proud of how he had defended the aid station, and he was glad to have him in his company. He called in Platoon Staff/Sergeant Bill Bennett and introduced Bettendorf to him. He related what Bettendorf had done. He said, "Bettendorf is to be treated as a regular and not as a replacement." He dismissed them and Sergeant Bennett led Bettendorf to his squad leader, Sergeant David Jones.

Sergeant Jones led a recon squad, and it was unusual for a replacement to be assigned to this squad. Of all the men that Bettendorf had been introduced to, Sergeant Jones would be one he would always remember.

The only thing that bothered Bettendorf was how he was going to keep in touch with Lillian. He needn't have worried about this, for as soon as Lillian learned about his transfer, she immediately found his address. She sent him a letter. She told him her address and said how important it was to her that they keep in touch. This was the beginning of a long and dangerous period in their lives.

Sergeant Jones was very upset about Bettendorf being assigned to his unit. He considered his unit as being the most professional unit of the company, and he had required that all of its members be top quality soldiers. His troops were exposed to the greatest danger whenever his company was engaged in battle. They were always the leading squad whenever any aggressive action was demanded of Company A.

With this in mind, he rushed to the company headquarters and told his First Sergeant of his concerns. First Sergeant William Betts said, "David, I think you should talk to the Captain." Sergeant Jones entered his Captain's office, and after saluting requested permission of the Captain to talk about a serious matter. Captain Petrie knew what he was going to say, and when he finished presenting his concerns, Captain Petrie said, "I know all of the needs your unit must have in order to perform their missions. That is exactly the reason why I assigned Private Bettendorf to your unit." Jones, with respect, protested further saying, "Even though Bettendorf has proven himself to be a fighter, he knows nothing about stealth. As the Captain knows, that is exactly what is necessary in the execution of my squad's missions." Captain Petrie replied to Jones indicating that he had one week to train Private Bettendorf in stealth as they were returning to the front around Ormoc. He told Jones he was dismissed, and Jones saluted. He did an about face and left the Captain's office saying nothing to the First Sergeant. The First Sergeant smiled and continued with his work.

When Jones arrived back to his tent, he sought out Bettendorf. He angrily told him that he had one week to train him in stealth, and he was going to make dam sure that he didn't cause any harm to the other members of his squad when they were in battle. Bettendorf was irritated by his Sergeant's statements and said, "I know all about stealth. I have hunted all of my life, and I can stalk animals, who are more skillful in stealth than any human being I have ever met." This response startled Jones as he had not expected such a response from a replacement. He said to himself, "Maybe I will take a second look at this guy."

For the next week he pushed Bettendorf as hard as he could. He put him through all the stealth exercises he could conceive. Bettendorf succeeded in all of these exercises and performed much better than Jones thought possible.

At the end of the week, the Captain assembled the company and said, "We will leave early in the morning for the front lines." He further said he knew many of them had very little time to relax, so he was issuing to all personnel a four hour pass. This pass was effective from 1700 to 2100. He made this announcement at 1600 hours. This gave time for Bettendorf to get in touch with Lillian, so when 1700 arrived, they would lose no time in finding each other.

When the time arrived, he rushed to the perimeter of his camp and found Lillian waiting. To his surprise, Lillian rushed into his arms and gave him a firm kiss on his lips. It startled him, but he had no difficulty responding whole heartily. Lillian grabbed his arm, and they walked away giving an appearance for all to see that they were not just friends. The older veterans of his unit were surprised that a young replacement could attract such a beautiful young lady. The next four hours went like a dream. By the time it ended, he knew that he had found the girl that was going to be a part of his life forever. He told Lillian this, and she said, "This is my feeling, too." When they parted, they gave each other a long tender kiss that promised much.

CHAPTER 4

The next morning, they loaded onto trucks and entered the road that led to Ormoc. Ormoc was about 30 miles from Tacloban, and in about two hours, they arrived at the front lines. As they approached the front, gun fire became very loud. Bettendorf looked and saw a P-51 airplane apparently engaged in a dog fight. Suddenly, it spun out of control and plunged straight down. It exploded when it hit the ground. He knew the pilot was killed as there was not a parachute. This was the first time he had seen an American killed.

Sergeant Jones quickly formed up his squad and reported to his platoon Lieutenant to find out if there were orders for his recon squad. He was told that his squad would do a night patrol with the object being to determine the strength and weakness of the opposing Japs. Jones still had deep concerns about Bettendorf. He explained to his squad their mission and drew Bettendorf aside reviewing with him all they had done in the past week. Essentially, he wanted his men to be spread out in a line parallel to the Japanese front lines. They were to advance, keeping each member in that parallel position. Bettendorf was to be at the extreme right. Bettendorf didn't understand the need for this formation, but he was determined to perform as directed. They advanced slowly being aware they might be walking into mines, or the Japs might suspect they were inspecting their lines and send up a flare to expose their positions. Sergeant Jones had warned them of the effect of the bright light on night vision. They were to close their eyes, so when the flare burned out, they would still have night vision. As they drew near to the Japanese front lines, Bettendorf heard two Japanese soldiers talking. He didn't understand what they were saying. He was aware that they seemed relaxed and had no idea of his presence. He broke his parallel position and worked behind them. When he got into a position to strike, he tensed up his muscles and sprang. These two Japanese soldiers had their heads close together, so they could whisper to each other. He quickly knocked them unconscious, and immediately disabled their machine gun. He put gags in their mouths and bound their hands behind them. He dragged them from their emplacement and tried to form up with his parallel. While all of this was happening, Sergeant Jones realized that Bettendorf was not in his parallel. He began cursing to himself and saying, "I knew it would happen as Bettendorf is performing just like a raw recruit." He broke away and worked toward Bettendorf's supposed position and arrived at this position just as Bettendorf was dragging his two Japanese soldiers to his position. Jones could not believe what he was seeing. Bettendorf had captured two prisoners, and he had single handedly subdued them. He quickly reorganized his patrol and hurriedly returned to his lines. Sergeant Jones and his squad immediately took their prisoners to S3 for interrogation. Bettendorf asked Jones if he could stay and witness the interrogation. Bettendorf had always been a "think ahead" guy. As he listened to the interrogation, he decided that he was going to learn how to speak Japanese.

As the interrogation proceeded, it became obvious that they were facing only a rear guard unit, and that the bulk of General Suzuki's forces had abandoned Ormoc.

A week prior to the above event, General Suzuki had received new orders from Commanding General Yamashito. He was instructed to save his troops and abandon Ormoc. Furthermore, he was told that the Japanese forces in the Philippines would receive no replacements. Their task now was to hold as many American troops in place as possible. This action would prolong the war, and possibly Japan could get better peace terms. General Suzuki successfully executed his evacuation without the Americans being aware. It was only Bettendorf's capture that alerted the Americans to what had happened. General Suzuki was further ordered, by any means, to go to Mindanao and take over command of the Japanese troops stationed there. His only means of doing this were by a small sailboat. A larger craft would most likely be spotted by the American Navy. Unfortunately, his small boat was caught in a severe storm and capsized. Suzuki drowned. One of Japan's best tactical Generals was lost.

When the above intelligence was revealed to the higher command, troops were ordered to advance, and they quickly swept aside the rear guard and occupied Ormoc. Jones was immensely proud of Bettendorf and praised him to all his fellow Sergeants. Captain Petrie heard about this and just smiled.

After the capture of Ormoc, the First Battalion was ordered to rejoin their 132nd regiment, who was already fighting on Luzon. As they were packing to leave Leyte, they received an order to send Bettendorf to infantry O.C.S. (Officers Candidate School) in Australia. When Bettendorf finished his basic training, he was selected to go to infantry officers training in the United States. His order to go to O.C.S. had not caught up with him until this point. There was one new condition to this order. He was to sign up for five years of post war duty. Bettendorf agreed, and he was immediately ordered to report to Tacloban, so he could fly to Australia. Bettendorf was excited about going to Tacloban as he knew he was going to see Lillian again. Before he left, Sergeant Jones and Captain Petrie asked him to request to return to their unit when he graduated from O.C.S. and was to be reassigned.

Lillian was sitting at her desk thinking about her intense feelings for Charles. She had always been a cautious person. It surprised her that she would have such strong feelings for Charles. They had been together only two times. How could this happen? Her first thought was of his physical appearance. She had first seen him in the aid station. She knew he was interested in her, but all she saw in him at that time was a teenage replacement. She had no interest in him. Then came that terrible morning. She had forgotten some of her equipment at the aid station and was irritated with herself for having to go there to retrieve it. She hardly noticed Charles and was going about her business when, suddenly, gun fire burst out all around her. Charles was dragging her to a corner of the aid station where there were some large boxes. He shoved her to the ground and started firing a rifle. She raised up and glimpsed Japanese soldiers advancing onto the aid station. They were firing at them. She felt a sudden panic. She found herself clinging to Charles. He gently pulled her hand from his firing arm and whispered, "Don't worry. We will be okay." She saw two Japanese soldiers fall and not move. There seemed too many of them for them to have any chance. This thought just led to more panic. Charles kept firing, and the soldiers seemed to be running past their position. She didn't understand this. She found herself growing numb, and everything went black. All the violent actions seemed to be like a dream in slow motion. The next moment she remembered was Charles holding her in his arms and trying to soothe her. She looked into his face and saw a caring concern. She began to hear his voice. He was telling her the danger was over, and she was safe. Slowly, she came out of her trancelike state and looked around. She saw dead Japanese soldiers around the aid station. It was then she realized what a tremendous fight Charles had done in their defense. She realized what she had thought was just another teenage soldier was really a very special soldier. As far as she was concerned, he was a strong and capable man. It was then she remembered how warm and caring he was during the intense struggle, that was all around them. She remembered thinking, "I must not let this man get away." The conversations they had after this ordeal confirmed all of her initial feelings and only intensified them. Having been reassured about her feelings, all she could think of was how she was going to keep in contact with him. She had given him her address and told him she wanted him to keep in touch with her. Would this be enough? She was hopeful.

As Charles was waiting for his three-quarter ton weapons carrier, he found himself thinking about Lillian. To him, Lillian was the most beautiful woman he had ever met. In his mind's eye he envisioned her. She was about five feet, six inches tall. Her body was well formed. She had a slim athletic build, but her curves were definitely feminine. She was blond headed with a reddish tint. Her eyes were a deep blue. To him, she was his movie star. Beyond all her good looks, he recognized a strong personality. The way she handled her supervisor when she scolded her for being with a soldier impressed him. He felt she was a person, who would stand up for what she believed. The way she greeted him on his last visit thrilled him. She had run up to him and kissed him warmly on his lips. How could he ever deserve a woman with all of these qualities? He was puzzling over this when his transportation arrived.

He told his driver that he had to stop by his old aid station to get some important things he had left behind. He didn't like lying, but he didn't think his driver would stop for him to see his girl. He didn't want him to know about Lillian. He wondered why he felt this way. Was he afraid of competition or did he feel that he didn't deserve her? The weapons carrier's gears engaged, and they turned onto the Ormoc-Tacloban road. What a difference two weeks made. Two weeks ago at this point, he could hear heavy gun fire. A few miles down the road, he saw the P-51 crash. After these memories, all of his thoughts were of Lillian and his hope that he could find her. He knew he had a short time to get to his air transport. Soon in the distance he saw the outskirts of Tacloban. The driver knew where the replacement depot was located and, suddenly, he was there. He jumped out of the vehicle and rushed to the aid station. Sergeant Maloney was there and he asked in a hurried voice if he had seen the Red Cross woman that worked out of the station. The Sergeant told him that she had just left and if he would hurry, he could see her walking to the post exchange. Charles rushed out, and he could see Lillian about two hundred feet away. He shouted loudly "Lillian" and started running towards her. Lillian heard his call and turned. She recognized him immediately and started running to him. They met and immediately embraced and kissed each other wildly. While still holding each other, they leaned back and Lillian asked how did he get to be here. He told her briefly about his Ormoc experience. Emphasizing his interest in learning to speak Japanese, he told her if she could speak Japanese, when the war was over, they could meet in Japan. This seemed farfetched to Lillian, but she said, "I will learn Japanese." He related that his delayed order to O.C.S. had arrived, and he was to go to Australia. She was impressed that he was going to be an officer. They talked about many things, and Charles said, "I know that we have just met, but I want you to know that you are the only woman I will ever love." These were the words Lillian wanted to hear, and she said that this was true for her. They seemed to glow in the meaning of what they both had said. Off in the distance, Charles heard his vehicle honking. He gave, and received, a long tender kiss from Lillian. It was a fond promising kiss. He ran for the vehicle, and the driver drove rapidly to the airport. The plane was loading, and Charles was just in time.

The plane he was to fly on was a C-46. It was referred to as the "Flying Bathtub". The plane took off without difficulty, and Charles found himself sitting in a very uncomfortable bucket seat. He really could not determine time as he had no watch. He had lost his watch capturing the two Japanese soldiers. He flew all the rest of the day. As dusk approached, he landed on an island called Biak. It was mid-February, 1945. This island had only been liberated for several months. There were no accommodations. He was issued K-rations and told he was to sleep on the tarmac under the wings of the C-46. It was a long night, and he slept poorly. There was no breakfast, and they took off at sunrise. They were scheduled to fly to Finchhaven. It was more than 700 miles.

The C-46 cruised at about 150-180 miles per hour. It would take about six hours to get there. When they were three hours into the flight, the starboard engine started smoking and flames appeared. The pilot shut down this engine and announced that they had only one engine. He said their position was due east of Wewak. He further stated that if they looked to the west, they could see the shore structures of Wewak. He warned them that if the plane had to land, it would be a water landing, and they should not swim to the New Guinea shore. The Japanese 18th Army under the command of General Adachi had specific orders to take no prisoners. His six hour flight turned into an eight hour flight. Charles found himself talking to two fellows. One was an anti-aircraft replacement, who was going to Saidor. Charles had never heard of this place. The other person was going to infantry O.C.S. as was he. They didn't have any significant conversation as they were constantly aware of their predicament. They were very sensitive to the sound of the remaining motor and maintained this alertness for the next four hours. The plane finally landed in Finchhaven, and they spent the night there. There were only tent accommodations with cots. These were okay, but without mosquito nets, he was easy prey to the mosquitoes. He was constantly swatting mosquitoes. About mid-day, he took off for Port Moresby. While flying over the Owen Stanley Mountains, he could make out some trails. These were the trails that the Japanese used when they tried to capture Port Moresby by land. These mountains were seven to eight thousand feet high. His plane flew close to ground level as there was no oxygen aboard. He stayed only a few hours in Port Moresby and flew to Cairns, Australia. Cairns was in the northern part of Queensland. It was near "No Man's Land". It was called this because the climate and the terrain were very incompatible for human beings. It had terrain comparable to the jungles of Luzon.

Charles was met at the plane by personnel from the O.C.S. station. They took him to the admission building, and he was interviewed. The main purpose of the interview was to determine what battle experience the new men had. Charles found out for the first time that Sergeant Jones had written the description of his battle experiences. It was only two incidents, but to read Jones' description, one would think Charles was an old veteran. The staff pondered in what group Charles should be put. There were several groups to consider. It came down to whether to put him in a non-battle group or a battle tested group. One of the members of the selection committee knew Sergeant Jones. He told the group that Sergeant Jones was a very demanding combat Sergeant. If he considered Charles to be a combat veteran, he would accept him as one. The group concurred, and Charles was assigned to a combat veterans group.

CHAPTER 5

The training for non-combat troops consisted of a more intensive basic training. The combat veterans had strenuous physical training, but they received more instruction in infantry tactics, particularly concerning the platoon level of combat. Charles was interested in this experience, but because he had been surrounded by Japanese soldiers at the aid station, he wanted to study how paratroopers managed what he called a "360 degree offense-defense situation". His instructors had no information for him. They gave him permission to use their training library. Charles found himself reading strategies of Clausevitz, Napoleon, famous Roman battles, and numerous others. None answered his questions. He decided he was going to have to figure this out with his own ideas of how he would perform in these circumstances.

He, also, was able to begin studying how to speak Japanese. Charles' interest pleased his instructors but at the same time, puzzled them. He was like no other candidate. He was top of his class in all of the subjects that were offered him. For a time, they considered retaining him on their staff. When they approached him about this possibility, he declined as he wanted to return to his old unit. He had an emotional connection with Captain Petrie and Sergeant Jones.

All during the time he was at O.C.S., he wrote daily to Lillian and to Sergeant Jones. It was obvious why he wrote to Lillian, but it was a different reason for Sergeant Jones. He wanted Sergeant Jones to keep him informed about where his old unit was and what type of combat they were having. Sergeant Jones told him that the Second and Third Battalions had fought in Manila and the Ipo Dam Site. Ipo Dam supplied the water for Manila. In his letter of mid-April, he reported the First Battalion was fighting the remnants of the Shembu group in the southeastern peninsula of Luzon. Charles knew nothing about Yamashito's groups and went immediately to the library and found that Yamashito had formed three groups of Japanese soldiers to defend Luzon. The Shobo group was to defend northern Luzon. The Kembu group defended Clark Field. The Shembu group, along with naval units, were to defend Manila and the southeastern peninsula. When Charles would rejoin his unit, they would be fighting holding actions of the Shembu group, who had about 50,000 troops. The last two weeks of his O.C.S. training ended. He had studied about how to attack defensive positions that were intended for hold and retreat.

His letters to Lillian were of a different nature. They were love letters, and as the days of separation lengthened, he felt more intense longings for her. At every mail call, he eagerly waited for her letters. All too often, none arrived. One day he would receive a bundle of letters. Lillian talked of her love for him and about her daily activities. In late April, she reported that they were shutting down the Leyte replacement center, and she was to be sent to a rest and recreation facility located in Manila. This thrilled Charles as he knew his unit was fighting southeast of Manila. He told her he hoped that he could see her soon.

At the end of his O.C.S. training, Charles was commissioned a Second Lieutenant. At the graduation ceremony, awards were given. Charles took them all. The O.C.S. staff again asked him to stay. He refused, and at his request, he was assigned to Company A. Now, he could return to Captain Petrie and Sergeant Jones. Captain Petrie admired him for his courage and his ability to be effective under fire. Sergeant

Jones admired him for his stealth. He also had grown fond of Charles as they had written each other numerous times during Charles' absence. Sergeant Jones was 38 years old. He felt that he had found a son in Charles.

CHAPTER 6

The flight back to Luzon was uneventful. This time he flew on a C-54. There were regular seats, and he could sleep most of the time. They had two stops for refueling. It was a continuous flight. It was around 2,000 miles from Cairns to Clark Field, Luzon. Clark was a functioning air field. He got off the plane and walked to the building for transients. Much to his surprise, there was Bill Williams. Captain Petrie had sent Bill to pick him up. This time Bill had a different attitude. Captain Petrie had given him a two day pass, and he had spent his time at the recreation and relaxation (R & R) center in Manila. When Lillian had heard that a Bill Williams from the 132nd Infantry Regiment was there, she found him and gave him a letter for Charles. In the letter she hoped that he would stop and see her when he was going to join his outfit.

Bill gave him Lillian's letter. Charles was very surprised and elated. He told Bill that he was going to issue his first order as a Second Lieutenant. They were stopping at the R & R. It was about an hour drive to the R & R, which was located on the eastern edge of Manila. Bill knew where Lillian would be located and took Charles to her. The feelings they had when they met could only be described as tumultuous. They embraced and couldn't be satisfied with their kisses. Bill was amazed by their passion. He wondered if he would ever experience the passion they had. They left Bill and went into Lillian's office. In the next few minutes, they tried to express all of their pent up emotions. They realized it was an impossible task. Charles could only stay a short time, and time seemed to be a second. Soon, Bill knocked on the door, and Charles knew he had to leave. Lillian was crying, and Charles was red faced. Tears came to his eyes. He would feel a deep sadness for the rest of his ride to Company A.

Charles entered the tent that was the headquarters of Company A. First Sergeant Betts immediately rose and saluted Second Lieutenant Bettendorf. This was Bettendorf's second salute from an enlisted man. Sergeant Betts told Bettendorf that the Captain was waiting for him. Bettendorf entered through the canvas partition and walked towards his Captain. He gave a smart salute and reported for duty. Captain Petrie returned his salute. He told Bettendorf to be at ease and extended his hand. As they talked, Bettendorf asked if he could command the platoon to which Sergeant Jones' recon unit was assigned. Petrie told him that Sergeant Jones had made the same request. He continued by reminding him that this platoon was the platoon that took the lead in any offensive action. Bettendorf said, "Sergeant Jones and I have corresponded all during the time I was at O.C.S., and we have discussed tactics. I feel we are a good fit." Petrie said, "Yesterday, his unit had come upon a defensive position that is going to be difficult to penetrate. The terrain is very rugged, and the enemy has good fields of fire. Furthermore, it is going to be difficult to flank. The holding and retreating actions of the Japanese are causing a marked increase in casualties." Sergeant Jones had been telling him the same thing for the past four weeks. He still wanted the assignment. Petrie was going to lose the Second Lieutenant that currently commanded this platoon. He was being reassigned to headquarters company. This action left an opening, so Bettendorf would command this platoon.

When he went to his platoon, he told his platoon Sergeant he wanted to observe how the platoon fought as they were going to attack this difficult defensive position that very morning. He met with Sergeant Jones. He told him he wanted him to be his special assistant as well as leading the recon squad. The assault was repulsed that day. He noticed that his men had to navigate a large open field to engage the enemy. He met with his platoon Sergeant and Sergeant Jones and said, "I feel that the only way to avoid heavy casualties is to attack at night." The platoon Sergeant said, "It is hard to direct a platoon in a night action. It is hard to control the action." Charles had read about how the paratroopers identified their men in a night action by using tiny snappers. A single click would be an enlisted man; a double, a non com; and a triple, an officer. After chow when it was dark, he took ten men from the platoon. He ran through a maneuver to see how effective they worked. He realized this idea would take too long to be effective with the current situation.

After that failure of the first attack, it was decided that the next day they would try a heavy artillery barrage on the defenses. By this time, Charles had become proficient in understanding the Japanese language. He asked Petrie if he and Jones could do a night patrol to see if he could pick up any conversations of Japanese soldiers. Petrie agreed. As he waited for night to come, he wrote a long letter to Lillian. He said, "I want to marry you, and I am constantly thinking of how much I long to be with you." Continuing, he said, "I want you to be engaged to me." He asked her to ask the post exchange manager if he knew of a jeweler in Manila that sold engagement rings. A few days later he received Lillian's answering letter. It was yes to everything.

It was dark when he finished his letter. He and Jones started their patrol. They went the length of the Japanese line without hearing anything. They repeated. This time it was close to midnight. They were in the middle of the line. Bettendorf heard Japanese soldiers talking. They talked about how badly damaged was their part of the defense line. They said if their sector was attacked, they would be overwhelmed. Bettendorf and Jones returned quickly to their lines and reported their findings. Bettendorf wanted to lead his platoon in the next day's attack and was given permission to do so. The attack was a success, and the Japanese were forced to retreat. The most important part of this victory was that they had no casualties. This amazed the men in his platoon as they had some fear of the new Lieutenant's ability. For several days they advanced only to be stopped by another defense line. Captain Petrie followed Bettendorf's advice and ordered a strong artillery strike on their defense line. He and Jones went on patrol that night. This time, Bettendorf heard them saying that their defense structure was compromised by the artillery barrage. They were just a rear guard defending it. This information was reported to Petrie and, again, Bettendorf led a successful attack.

After this attack, the battalion commander asked Petrie to report to his headquarters He took Bettendorf with him. Petrie related the reason for their success. The battalion commander asked Bettendorf if he had any other ideas. He told about his idea of a 360 degree offense-defense combat team. He said, "At first, I wanted it to be platoon size. Now, I feel that in order to use it against Shembu's main line of defense, a company strength would be required." Lieutenant Colonel Joy, the battalion commander said, "I will report this to the regimental commander."

In a few days they came upon a much stronger blocking defense. The previous approach did not work. Bettendorf came up with a different approach. He outlined it to Petrie in the following manner: He would pick out three points on the map of the area where the new defense line was located. These points, with accurate coordinates, would be fired upon by the artillery at specific times. They would, for example, fire two hours on point one, wait two hours and fire in the same number of hours on point two, and do the same on point three. All of this would begin at 2100. Bettendorf would position himself close to point one during the first artillery barrage and the other two in the same manner. He wanted to be at each position during the barrage. After a severe barrage, he might get information about their position. He felt the Japanese soldiers might be so unnerved by the barrage that they would talk with each other. This worked, and the following attack worked.

As a result of this action, two things happened. One, Bettendorf was put in and received a bronze star, and two, he captured a middle aged Japanese officer. This officer had been a professor of languages at the Tokyo Imperial University. He got permission from regimental headquarters to keep this prisoner at Company A. With this prisoner's help, he would become more proficient in speaking and reading the Japanese language.

That night he was busily writing Lillian. He was telling her how hard it was to be so close geographically to her but so far away in reality. He said, "At times I have sexual needs for you that are so great that it isn't unusual for me to have two or more wet dreams during the week." He had just finished that sentence when Petrie walked into his tent. He handed him a four day pass issued by the regimental colonel as a reward for his remarkable duty.

CHAPTER 7

Since it was late at night when he received his pass, he could not leave until morning. In the morning, he was issued a jeep and off he went. It took him two hours to go about 30 miles. He knew exactly where Lillian's office was, and he arrived just as she was leaving the building. They saw each other and rushed into each other's arms. Holding each other so tightly, they appeared to be trying to melt their bodies together. In this tight embrace, Lillian could feel his erect penis. It thrilled her. When the excitement lessened, they went into her office to try to catch up on all the days they had missed. He said, "I want to marry you immediately, but if we do, you will be sent home to the States. I want to have a personal marriage, a marriage where we exchange our vows in private and no one would know we are married but ourselves." He asked further if she had found out about a ring. She said, "Yes, to all." All he had to do was to go to the post exchange and buy it. He immediately got up and literally dragged her to the exchange. He was walking so fast. When they got back to her office, they exchanged vows. As he put the ring on her finger, he said, "With this ring, I thee wed." In two short hours much had happened in their lives. Lillian said, "I know you have sexual tensions, but I want us to wait until night to consummate our marriage." She wanted them to talk more together as they had only three physical contacts and four months of letters since they had met each other. He regretted the delay, but he realized the value of her request. With that in mind, they went for a walk. They found it was easy for them to talk. She wanted to talk about her family and what her life was like before she met him. It seemed to him that she had a loving family. Her father was away much of the time due to his military service. She related about his being wounded in the North African campaign. He was leading a battalion of infantry at Kasserine Pass. Rommel's tank corp overwhelmed the tank brigade that his battalion was supporting. Lillian's dad said that tanks and infantry don't mix well. Her father was severely wounded and was hospitalized for nine months. He got a medical discharge. She felt the family compensated for his being away and endured his recovery. She told many stories about her childhood and all of the years that led up to their meeting.

It became his turn. He told her he was reluctant to talk about his life and his family. She said, "You know how important it is for me to know all about your life. I am going to be with you all of my life." Charles responded by telling his life story. He said, "From the age of four until I was fifteen years old, my family experienced the depression. My parents, during this period grew apart, and my father started drinking and began an affair. My mother ignored this and became very passive. She did nothing. She passively endured. I felt I survived by studying and by hunting. This kept me away from home much of the time. Most of my life I have wanted to be a doctor, and at age 16, I started pre-med. I was finishing my second year when I entered the Army. The rest you know." She knew that there was much more to tell, but she saw how hard it was for him to go over his past. She was ready to go on to other things.

They talked about things that came to mind. Just before they went to supper, he told her about his bronze star. She was surprised at the casualness of his remark. If it had happened in her family, there would have been much excitement. She thought there is much to know about this man.

After supper Charles realized their consummation was near. He started to remind himself he must move slowly. He didn't want his demands to ruin their first sexual experience. This was strictly his concern as Lillian was very excited about having sex. They went to her room. She had only a cot for her bed. A pallet was put on the floor, and she went into the bathroom to change her clothes. Charles immediately undressed and waited for her. He was completely naked. After what seemed an eternity, the door to the bathroom opened. Lillian stood before him without her clothes. To him, it was the most beautiful body he had ever seen. They crossed the room pressing their bodies together while they kissed deeply and passionately. Charles slowly picked her up and gently laid her on the pallet. He did this without losing their passionate kiss. He was at her side, and he ran his hand along her body ending up caressing her vagina. As their tension increased, he gently spread her legs and moved between them. Lillian couldn't take her eyes off his body, and she marveled at the size of his penis. She felt an eagerness for it. As he leaned forward to embrace her more closely, she reached up and grasped his penis. She wanted to feel it and was surprised that she could feel it throb. Laying down on top of her, he supported his body with his elbows, so she would feel no restriction of movement. Their kisses were now more intense and he slowly began inserting his penis. At first, he felt some resistance, and Lillian jerked a little, but they both were so involved they hardly noticed. Charles began slowly plunging in and out. Shortly, the sensation was so great that he began pumping more rapidly, and Lillian was responding with flexing her hips, so she could meet his thrust. Rapidly, the sensation became so very intense that they could hardly stand it. Charles' penis seemed to explode, and the outside part of her vagina began to rapidly contract. They temporarily lost consciousness. Slowly, their orgasms abated, and they found their mouths locked together. They were both holding tightly to the other's buttocks in order to keep his penis in her vagina. They said how much they loved each other and went to sleep. They had sex several times that night, but by 2:00 a.m., they were exhausted and slept soundly in each other's arms. When they awakened, they found his penis was still in her vagina. They lay on their sides and talked. Slowly, his penis became hard, and they had early morning sex.

They slept for about 50 minutes, and then they got up and showered. Both wanted to soap and wash their partner's genitals. It seemed to them they were in a different fantastic world. The rest of his leave was a glorious honeymoon. When he parted to return to his company, they felt that a part of their selves was being torn away.

CHAPTER 8

When he arrived back with his company, he found they had advanced to a well established defensive line of the Shembu group. This was not a hold and retreat defense line. This apparently was going to be their last stand. There were obvious geographic reasons for this. If they retreated further, they would be trapped in the peninsula. By making a stand here, they still had a land connection with Yamashito's forces in the Sierra Madre Mountains. It was now late July, 1945. Both sides sensed that the war was about over. The Americans were reluctant to attack as it meant casualties. The end seemed so near. Germany had been defeated and had accepted unconditional surrender terms on May 8, 1945. Japan had been offered the same terms. The battle for Okinawa had been costly on both sides. Iwo Jima had cost the marines 25,000 casualties. Japan was trying to get Stalin to continue their non-aggression treaty. Stalin had refused to resign their non-aggression pact, and Russian forces were building up along the Manchurian border. They would attack in August. An internal fight was going on in the Japanese government. Those people, who were for peace at any cost, were being overwhelmed by militants. Because of these unsettling developments, Washington decided to put as much pressure on Japan as possible. Hence, the 132nd infantry was ordered to attack.

Bettendorf's idea that a company as a unit could fight aggressively when they were surrounded (he called it an aggressive-defensive assault team) was approved by regimental headquarters. Captain Petrie and First Lieutenant Bettendorf were to mold Company A into this kind of an assault team. Bettendorf and Sergeant Jones were responsible for teaching stealth. The first problem they ran into was the fear the men had of intentionally allowing the enemy to surround them. It became Captain Petrie's job to convince them that they could fight, over a short period of time, the enemy on all points of the compass. The term "short period of time" concerned them as it sounded as if they might be sacrificed. Petrie was going to be honest with them. He pointed out to them that in battle no one could predict the outcome. He said he and Bettendorf had studied this approach for a long time, and they both thought it would work. The men had three experiences with Bettendorf's ideas, and they knew his plans had saved many of their lives. This reassured them, and they became excited about this way of fighting. In two weeks they were ready. The complete plan was laid out to the entire company. It went as planned.

The battle began with a strong artillery barrage along the entire battle line. This was to weaken their defenses. After two hours of pounding the enemy, the guns were to shift to the center section of the line where Company A was located. The guns then started a rolling forward artillery barrage with Company A following closely behind the barrage. When the barrage was directly on the enemy's defense lines, the barrage was to stop. Company A was on top of the enemy. They broke through and advanced forward in a manner that convinced the enemy that they could be cut off and destroyed. The enemy troops that were needed to close the gap would have to come from their lines on either side of the gap. The forward advance of Company A had brought forward and engaged the enemy's reserves. This would weaken their defense line and leave no reserves to commit. This made them more vulnerable to the attacking Americans. Company A attacked when the encirclement was completed. They used their attack defense mode and attacked the Japanese soldiers that had closed the gap. These Japanese soldiers were in a vulnerable position as they had no defensive structures to fight from. This exposure gave the heavy fire power of Company A an advantage that overwhelmed the opposing forces. The strong attacks of the Americans on a weakened enemy line led to a rout, and the Shensu group would no longer be an organized force. All that was left were isolated groups of die hard Japanese troops. The battle was fought just as Bettendorf had predicted. The regimental command was very pleased by this outcome and awarded both Petrie and Bettendorf a silver star. This battle ended on August 2, 1945.

On August 8, 1945, Hiroshima was bombed with an atom bomb. One week later, an atom bomb was dropped on Nagasacki. From the 15th of August to the 20th, the Japanese government was in turmoil.

President Truman decided to have another bomb made and delivered. The Japanese peace group persuaded the Emperor to broadcast a message to his people that the unthinkable had happened, and the Japanese must accept the inevitable and surrender. This was taped and was to be broadcast the next day. The tape was hidden and for a good reason. General Amuri and his co-conspirators planned to attack the Imperial Palace. They would capture the tape and seize the Emperor. They intended to get him to change his mind. The attackers could not find the tape, and the Emperor was not captured. General Amuri committed hari-kiri. The revolt was over.

Two Betty Bombers with large green crosses on their sides were dispatched to the Philippines. They brought orders to Yamashito that he was to submit to unconditional surrender.

The 132nd infantry regiment was ordered to load up and to prepare to travel to Batangas where they would board a landing ship tank (LST) for Japan. Charles knew that he would pass close to Lillian and asked Petrie if he could stop for a few minutes to be with Lillian and tell her goodbye and where he was going. Petrie went to regimental headquarters and asked permission for Bettendorf to leave early, so he would have a day with his fiancee'. This request was granted. He was supposed to meet their convoy the next day on the outskirts of Manila. He left immediately and in no time he was with Lillian. They had another honeymoon, and he told her, what had been happening to him. Again, he just casually mentioned that he had received a Silver Star and was a First Lieutenant. Lillian was again amazed about Charles. He had a promotion to First Lieutenant and got a Silver Star. He didn't seem to think this was big news. His big news was being with Lillian. They had a wonderful day. The day was soon over, and it looked like very soon they would be together forever. He told Lillian that he was going to use his skill in speaking the Japanese language to help him position himself for his post-war duty in the Army. He told Lillian about his having to sign up for five years post war duty in order to go to O.C.S. He again told her to continue her Japanese language studies as he saw that this would be a way of keeping her near him while he was in Japan. The time passed quickly, and he found himself waiting by the road side for his unit. He connected, and before he knew it, they were on board a LST and were at sea.

CHAPTER 9

As the ship was pulling away from the sight of land, Bettendorf wondered why he was interested in speaking Japanese. The first thought seemed the best reason. When he was sneaking up on the Jap soldiers outside of Ormoc, he heard them talking. He was frustrated that he could not understand what they were saying. He realized that if he could learn the language, then he would be in a one up position. When he asked himself why he was interested in a 360 degree battle team, he remembered how it was at the battle for the aid station. He remembered he was firing in all directions. He was successful and thought it could apply for a larger group. This became a problem solving issue for him. He decided that he must like complex problems.

He thought it was going to be an uneventful voyage, but this was not to be. When he was opposite Okinawa, his LST ran into a typhoon. Quickly, his ship was experiencing one hundred foot high waves. The ship would go up the wave to its peak. As it flattened on the top of the peak, the propeller would rise out of the water and whirl rapidly. This would shake the ship violently. Many thought the ship would sink. As usual, Bettendorf showed no anxiety. After four hours, the waves lessened, and they sailed on to Japan.

It was early one morning when he spotted Mt. Fuji. It was a perfect cone with a top of white snow. To Bettendorf it was a spectacular sight. They were only sixty miles from Tokyo. They were to attend the surrender ceremonies. After the ceremonies, he landed at Tateyama Naval Base, and he helped initiate their occupational duties. They were to disarm and demobilize numerous Japanese units and close their bases. In disabling Tateyama there was a tremendous explosion. There was much destruction and casualties. When the destruction of this base was completed, they were to process returning Japanese soldiers. This would keep Charles busy for several months.

Charles had brought his Japanese officer with him. Up to this time, he had considered him an enemy and refused to say his name. Now he felt their relation could be different. He went to the Japanese officer's quarters on the boat. It was like a prison cell. Charles asked in Japanese what he was called when he was a civilian. He replied, "Professor Akihiko Okada." Okada said, "Actually, I was never really a civilian as the army kept me on active duty with detached duty assignment to the Tokyo Imperial University. When the war broke out with the United States, I was immediately attached to the 48th division of General Homma's 14th Army. I was to interrogate American and British prisoners. When Bataan fell, I was swamped with this duty. I was offended by the manner that all prisoners of war were treated. I was stationed in Manila. I would go periodically to the prison camps. The inhumanity was sickening. I made up my mind that if I ever had a chance, I would surrender to the Americans. I wanted no part of these animals with whom I was soldiering. You always thought that you captured me, but in reality, I sought you out in order to surrender. You treated me as a prisoner of war and assumed that I was a die-hard militarist that you could use in your effort to be a competent speaker in Japanese. Your treatment of me degraded me." After this outburst Bettendorf was reluctant to say anything. He knew that he would need him in his language school. He went on to say that when they reached Tokyo, he would be released. He continued saying, "I am going to organize a school to teach the Japanese language to American troops, who would be occupying Japan." He asked if he would want to be on his staff. Akihiko said, "I will think about it." He still felt anger about the way he had been treated while he was a prisoner. In the near future they would talk again.

After the regiment got settled in, they started fulfilling their responsibility to disarm the Japanese soldiers. Charles had spent a lot of time learning Japanese customs from Akihiko. He was particularly interested in how Japanese officers addressed each other. This ability was of tremendous help to his regiment as he knew how to be respectful but authoritative in his dealing with the hostile officers that were still strongly militant in their feelings against the surrender. He found that he had an ability to be persuasive. This surprised him. Soon his ability became well known in the Japanese Army and MacArthur's headquarters. The Japanese citizens had much resentment of the occupying forces, especially following the rape of Japanese women at the Atsugi Air Base. The American troops involved in these rapes were severely punished. This did little to lower the tension. The request for Bettendorf was a pleasant surprise. Nothing was done about it immediately as they had too many pressing matters. Charles had one important issue, and it was how to get Lillian to Japan.

He wrote repeatedly to Lillian about how important it was for her to learn Japanese. Lillian understood this, but all she had were the language books that Charles had sent her. They were no help in learning how to speak Japanese. As the military action ceased, and as the troops began to go home, Lillian's work shifted to taking care of Filipino refugees. The battle of Manila had caused 100,000 civilian deaths and had led to a massive separation of Filipino families. Lillian was asked to set up a place where Filipinos could come and register their names and where they could be contacted. This would be a way to reconnect the Filipino families. Lillian had an ability to learn languages rapidly, and she started learning Tagalog. Many Filipinos could speak English but speaking Tagalog helped in many cases. Her ability was noted by many Filipinos and came to the attention of Isabella Hernandez. Isabella was (prior to the war) the personal maid to the wife of a Japanese military attache' in the Japanese embassy. The embassy was in Manila. Isabella was very loyal to her mistress. When war was declared, she was of great help to her Japanese family as they had a hard time before the Japanese troops arrived. In return, the family took care of Isabella and her family during the Japanese occupation. When war again came, the husband became assigned to the Navy and was killed in the battle for Manila.

When this Japanese military attache' realized that the Japanese Army was not going to prevail, he went to Aiko, his wife, and said he could not help her. She would have to take care of herself and the children. The bitterness he felt for her and the children came out. She had not given him a male child, and he felt that she had failed him in all manners. He said a bitter goodbye. Isabella heard this conversation and was shocked. When Aiko, her mistress, asked her if she would help her escape from Manila, she was glad to help. Isabella loved this family and immediately moved them to a remote area where they would be protected by her family. This action saved her Japanese family, but now they wanted to go to Japan. Isabella had heard that Lillian was trying to learn Japanese, and she thought that this might be a way to get Aiko home to Japan.

Lillian listened carefully to her story, and immediately knew this was the break she needed in order to learn Japanese. She told Isabella that she definitely was interested in helping Aiko. The condition was that she teach her Japanese -- not only the Japanese language, but also Japanese customs. She especially wanted to know diplomatic customs. She really didn't know what problems she was getting into. Lillian just wanted to be able to fit into the highest level of Japanese society. She, like Charles, liked to think ahead. First, she had to arrange for a safe place for Aiko and the girls.

Some of her friends were helpful. It was possible for Aiko, her two daughters, and Isabella to move in with her. It would be very crowded, but all were very happy with this arrangement. With Aiko there, she learned Japanese very rapidly. With Aiko's help, she wrote her next letter to Charles in Japanese. Charles was greatly surprised. He had to get help reading it as Aiko had used Japanese symbols he didn't know. When he finished reading the letter, all he could say was "wow". He was immensely proud of Lillian's accomplishment. He knew now he had a bigger problem. He had five people to get to Japan.

CHAPTER 10

When Akihiko got to Japan, he had made up his mind that he would not be able to get over his anger about his prisoner of war treatment. He told Charles he would not accept his offer to join his language school. He didn't talk about his anger. He said, "I must find my family, and I want to start back teaching at Tokyo University." The word "Imperial" had been dropped from the title. He had no idea of the destruction of Tokyo and Yokohama. When he left Charles, he was immediately confronted by this destruction. The fire storm following the incendiary raids had destroyed Tokyo University. His old neighborhood was gone. He had no idea where his family was or if he did have a family. He searched his neighborhood hoping to find a survivor. There simply was no one there. His only hope was to go to where his wife had relatives. They lived in Kyoto. Kyoto was quite a distance from Tokyo. He had no hope of getting there as the railroad system was in shambles. He knew that the only chance he had was Charles. He knew he was going to have to find some way to deal with his anger. A more immediate problem was that he had no shelter and no access to food. He went to Tateyama Naval Base hoping Charles was still there.

Charles' outfit had left and no one knew where. It looked hopeless. As he was walking out of the base, he ran into a Japanese officer, who had just been returned to Japan from the Philippines. He was talking about what a great experience he had. He was interviewed by an American officer, who could speak perfect Japanese. Akihiko had not been listening to his friend as he felt so desperate about his situation. When he heard an American officer speaking perfect Japanese, he immediately was all ears to his friend. He forgot Japanese politeness and interrupted him. In a frantic and demanding tone, he said, "Where is this officer?" The officer gave him the address where the American officer was interviewing returning Army officers.

MacArthur's headquarters had decided Bettendorf interviewing would be a resource of information in connection with returning Japanese officers, who were involved in guerilla activities. This is why he was away from his outfit and in Tokyo. Akihiko found Charles and went through a formal Japanese apology with Charles. Charles was surprised to see Akihiko so soon. He was aware of how shabby he looked, and it was obvious that he had lost weight. Akihiko decided he would tell Charles the exact reason for his seeking him out. He started talking about his family and his inability to find them. He related that his university was destroyed, and he had no work. He said, "My only possible way to find my family is to go to Kyoto. Besides all of this, I am starving." Charles was sympathetic about Akihiko's plight, but his only interest in him was his language ability, and he needed to know if he would commit to being in his language school. Akhiko replied that he realized that was the only thing he had to offer that would encourage Charles to help him.

With this yes, Charles immediately got some food for Akihiko and moved him into his quarters. It so happened that Charles was to go to Kyoto the next day, and he agreed to take Akihiko with him. He further said, "I will drive you around the Kyoto area and help you find your family." This led to an involved search. They did find his wife and his two daughters (Chiase, age 14 and Chie, age 7). Akihiko's joy was poignant. Even though Charles knew both had strong emotional feelings for each other, they just bowed to each other and did not hug or kiss. This was not true of the two girls as they rushed into their Father's arms and hugged and kissed him. Charles knew that Akihiko and his wife would have their welcoming in private. Akihiko and his wife, Ayame, had thought that the other was dead. This reunion was a miracle to them. Needless to say, Akihiko and his family would be forever indebted to Charles.

That night after Akihiko and Ayame had settled down the children, they had a long talk. Akihiko wanted to know, what happened while he was overseas. Ayame said, "The girls and I moved in with my parents. Things went pretty well until April 18, 1942. On that day, the Americans bombed Tokyo. It didn't do much damage, but it scared all of us as we felt that we were going to get bombed. Actually, nothing happened for a few years. The only thing we noticed about the war was that it got harder and harder to get basic foods. This only got worse. Initially, the workers in military plants got extra rations. By 1945, we were all on near starvation rations. We tried to grow vegetables and any other food that we could think of. 1945 was the worst time. On the 19th of February, we had a bombing of the Tokyo Port. On the 25th of February, we had our first incendiary bombing raid. Those kind of bombing attacks continued to happen. We thought about getting out of Tokyo. We had not been hit by the fire bombs, so we thought we might be in an area that would not be bombed. Mother and Dad were very weak at this time as they would give part of their rations to the girls. They could not have traveled. On May 9th and 10th, we were burned out. Mother and Dad were too weak to run, and they told us to run to the River Sumida. We stayed as long as we could, and then we ran. I looked back and saw the flames suck up people. We got to the river, and the water was hot. At one time the flames were so intense that we felt that we had no oxygen to breathe. After the fire, we went to Kyoto. It was a horrible trip. We were very weak when we found our relatives. We knew that we had lost the war, and all we could do was to pray for peace and your return." As she was telling this to Akihiko, he could see the terror in her eyes. At the end, she started crying. He could not console her. Finally, in exhaustion, they went to sleep. Neither one had thought of having sex.

Charles had an immediate problem of where to house all these people. He had no idea how he was going to do it. He pondered this all the way back to Tokyo. As soon as he arrived, he called Captain Petrie and discussed the problem with him. Petrie had no solution to the problem. He said, "MacArthur's headquarters needs you, and all you have to do is to impress them of the value of Akihiko. They will work out the details." Charles didn't believe this, but he felt that it was the only option he had. He went to his immediate superior and made his request. He conveyed in strong terms the qualities of Akihiko and the fact that he had been a professor of Japanese language at Tokyo University. His superior had to pass it up the chain of command. Charles didn't know how long this would take and requested some way to take care of Akihiko and his family until a decision could be made. His superior knew how desperate conditions were for Japanese civilians and agreed to let Charles house them in his small quarters. So, here for the next few weeks, Charles was going to have a very hard time.

His request was approved, and with Akihiko's help, the organization and the staffing of the language school progressed rapidly. Charles found an abandoned girls' school in Yokohama and immediately confiscated it. This fit perfectly with his plans as it would offer quarters for his Japanese staff and rooms for lecturing. Another plus, the neighborhood the school was in was amazingly in good repair. An anti-aircraft unit was currently housed there. They had orders to move to Tomioka Sea Plane Base. There were no other problems about getting the quarters for his language school. With this and his good work with the militant Japanese officers, Bettendorf felt for the first time that he had enough influence to get Lillian to Tokyo.

Lillian wrote back that Aiko had been talking more to her about her family in Japan. She related that Aiko was the daughter of General Suzuki, who had been killed in the battle for Leyte. Aiko's husband had been a Naval attache' in the Japanese embassy before and during the war. He was killed leading a Naval assault in the battle for Manila. Her husband's name was Hideki (meaning splendid opportunity) Yamamoto. His uncle was Admiral Yamamoto. She hoped that this would help. She ended as they both did with expressions of love and wanting to be with him.

Charles was excited about the opportunities the information in her letter could mean for both of them. He happened to be at MacArthur's headquarters when he received this letter. He went immediately to the division that worked with the Japanese diplomatic service. When they learned about whom Bettendorf was talking, there was an immediate stir of action. General Suzuki and Admiral Yamamoto were highly respected men in Japan. The diplomatic service had been searching for Aiko and her two girls as soon as the surrender was implemented. Up to this point, they had not had any success. The diplomatic service immediately notified both families and went to MacArthur's headquarters. They wanted to convey the importance of this find to these Japanese families as well as to the nation. Both men, Suzuki and Yamamoto, were highly honored in Japan. At this time, MacArthur didn't want any war heroes for the new Japan. They debated for several hours about what to do with this request for help.

Finally, they called in Lieutenant Bettendorf. Bettendorf knew of MacArthur's objection to war heroes, and he thought of a possible rebuttal that he might use if he was called to this meeting. He started with describing the difficulty of dealing with the humiliation and anger of Japanese authorities and ordinary citizens. He said, "I find that most of these people feel all they receive from the occupying forces are orders and humiliation." He proposed that this might be a break for them and might show some good will. They were helping a poor, helpless widow with two daughters to come home. He said, "We don't have to emphasize their relatives. The Japanese will know, who she is, and will recognize the subtlety. They will be impressed by our handling of this matter because they would have handled it that way if they were victors."

The diplomatic group and MacArthur's staff were impressed by the astuteness of this Lieutenant. They dismissed him and did not indicate what they intended to do. Charles left feeling he had lost a great opportunity to get Lillian to Tokyo.

CHAPTER 11

After he left, they ordered the Army to assist the Suzuki and Yamamoto families in any way they could. In a letter to the Japanese government, they stated they wanted to get this poor, unfortunate widow and her two daughters back to Japan. As soon as this information was given to Aiko's families, plans were made to get Aiko home. With the request of the Japanese government, the Swiss embassy was asked to help in the extraction of Aiko and her two girls. They were glad to help as they wanted to have some influence with the new Japanese government.

One day later, a black limousine drove up and parked in front of Lillian's office. Two men in black suits with grey Stetson hats got out and approached her office. They would not identify themselves but insisted on talking to Miss Lillian Kenworth. The secretary was confused. She told them to have a seat, and she would ask if Miss Kenworth could see them. Lillian peaked through a partly closed door and saw these very official individuals. She feared that it was something to do with Aiko. She was determined to protect Aiko and the girls. She told the secretary to let them come in. The men entered and presented their credentials. She was surprised they were Swiss diplomats. She was immensely relieved as she was sure it had nothing to do with Aiko. The diplomats opened a letter from the Suzuki and the Yamamoto families. The letter said, "We have information you know the whereabouts of Aiko Yamamoto and her two daughters." Lillian was startled and refused to have anything else to do with them. They knew she was trying to protect Aiko, so they had another letter from General MacArthur's headquarters requesting her to do all she could to help these gentlemen. She stalled and said, "I will have to think about this request. You will need to come tomorrow." The men said that Aiko was in grave danger as they had sources that told them the Philippine secret police were searching for Aiko. Lillian believed them and asked if they could protect Aiko. They said, "That is why we have come immediately to your office as we want to get her and the two girls to their embassy as soon as possible." With this, Lillian left the office with these two men and took them to Aiko's hiding place. Aiko was terrified when Lillian walked in with these two official looking men. They quickly reassured her and showed the letters from her families. The Suzuki letter contained a secret symbol that was known only to the Suzuki family. With a gasp, she hugged both men and told Lillian the significance of the letter. The men told Aiko to get the two girls, and they would take them to the Swiss embassy. She insisted that Lillian and Isabella must come, also, or she would not go. This request was quickly accepted, and they left with nothing but themselves. As they pulled away, they passed a Filipino military police jeep headed towards Lillian's office. The Swiss flag on the car reassured the military police that they did not need to stop them. From that time until they drove into the embassy, there was much anxiety. The Swiss immediately contacted MacArthur's headquarters. They reported the incident with the Filipino military police. They were told it would be taken care of.

After the five women had settled and adjusted to their surroundings, they sat together in order to express their feelings concerning, what had just happened. Aiko said, "Before we begin, I want my two daughters, Asami and Akemi, to participate." Lillian had not spent much time with the girls. Even though they lived in the same apartment, her Red Cross duties started before they got up in the morning, and they were in bed when she returned at night. The girls came in. All started talking about how they felt over the sudden change in their lives. Lillian was exceedingly happy. She felt all she had to do was to resign from the

Red Cross and get ready to be with Charles. She had written a note to her commander saying she was resigning, and she would write a longer letter. Her letter was hand delivered by the Swiss embassy, and by their delivering it, her commander was reassured that she was okay.

Aiko was relieved. She was finally safe. She couldn't really grasp the feeling that she would be home again. She had been away for ten years. She had left Tokyo with a four year old girl, Akemi, and a two year old girl, Asami. They were now fourteen and twelve, respectively. Just a few months ago, they were involved in a violent battle for Manila. She had lost a husband. She had to hide from vengeful Filipinos and the American Army. Now this American Army was helping her to return home. All of this seemed unimaginable.

Isabella was the tearful one. She was leaving her home and her family. She knew that some of her people would consider her a traitor. She feared the Filipino government would punish her family. When she took Aiko to Lillian, she knew that she had committed her life to be with Aiko and the girls. She was strongly attached to the girls.

The girls were typical teenagers. They had been in a restricted life as long as they could remember, and now they just might be free. At that time, they said very little

In two days they were on a C-54 headed for Tokyo. Five returnees were having both their happiness and their fears. It was a ten hour flight, and they were to be met by Aiko's family. Charles had not been notified that Lillian was on that flight. MacArthur's headquarters had decided that Aiko would have a quiet return with no publicity. At that time they were very active in their censorship of information.

The return flight gave all of the women time to reflect on, what had happened to them. Lillian had a lot of questions for Aiko. She asked

Aiko why did she insist on her being a part of the group to go with the Swiss delegation. Before Aiko answered, she said, "I am so grateful that you did demand my coming." Aiko thought for a moment before she answered Lillian. She thought it wasn't because of her love for Lillian or for having an emotional dependence on her. Her next thought sounded exploitative, and she didn't want to offend Lillian. She said to herself, "Good relations could only be built on honest exchanges." She knew she would need Lillian's friendship in post war Japan. She said, "Lillian, my real motive for insisting that you come with me was because I did not trust the Swiss." Aiko had known them when her husband was with the Japanese embassy. The Japanese embassy staff felt that Switzerland was a small nation, and they survived by being manipulative. This meant to her that they would be more interested in their self interest than hers. If they were going to betray her, she felt Lillian would be an obstacle. They might not like betraying an American. She was using Lillian. She said, "If this has offended you, please forgive me." Lillian thought she really liked this woman. She has the courage to be honest with herself and with her. Lillian didn't say a word. She got up and hugged Aiko.

Lillian told Aiko if they were going to talk about exploiting, consider how Aiko had taught her Japanese language and customs. Lillian felt that Aiko had given her so many advantages that Charles would be able to find a place for her. Now, there would be no real danger that she would be sent home. Charles had told her that MacArthur was not going to let dependents come to Japan until the supply problems of the troops and the Japanese people were resolved. The tentative date was the end of January, 1946.

Aiko talked further about her concern about going home. She had no husband and her father was dead. How was she going to take care of her two girls? She had heard how much of Japan was destroyed. Had the homes of her family been destroyed? Of course, she had no answer. With this statement, all became silent and remained so for over an hour.

Suddenly, the silence was broken by Isabella crying. Her crying was still related to her feeling displaced, and a real concern that her family might be in danger. There was no way they could console her, so they let her cry it out.

Akemi, the fourteen year old, suddenly said, "I am glad to get to go to Japan. I have had no friends of my own age for practically all of my life. I have either been restricted by the embassy or by wars. Now is the time for me to live a normal life." This was not to happen for several years.

Asami, who was twelve, had said nothing. Her sister Akemi told her she was always talking to her about what she wanted, so speak up. All she could say was that she had always wanted a home like other kids. This was all she wanted.

They were silent for a couple of hours. All were in their own worlds. They were awakened from their revelries by a red flashing light as the pilot announced they were approaching Tokyo. They had nothing to carry, so all they did was to sit up and look out the windows. They were horrified by what they saw. It seemed that all of Tokyo was destroyed. They could see the imperial grounds and across the moat from the imperial grounds was the Dai-Ichi Mutual Life Insurance building. It was intact. This was General MacArthur's headquarters. Lillian thought this was where her Charles was working. Maybe he was there right this minute. The airplane landed in a few minutes and slowly taxied up to what might be called a terminal. Aiko and the girls got off first. They walked briskly to their waiting families. It had been a long time since Aiko had been with her families, so the reunion was formal. The women of the Suzuki family were the ones to break the ice, and they grabbed the girls and then Aiko. After greetings were over, Aiko introduced Lillian. Lillian responded in correct Japanese, and she addressed Aiko's families in a traditional manner, which was a great surprise to them.

Both families told Aiko that their homes in Tokyo were destroyed. They said, "We live in small houses on the outskirts of Tokyo." It was then Aiko asked, what would happen to Lillian. A Japanese diplomat said, "I will make arrangements for her." So, Lillian found herself alone with a Japanese diplomat.

Since he realized that she spoke Japanese very well, he said, "I am aware that Charles' report to the MacArthur's headquarters is the main reason for Aiko's return to Japan." He further said the Japanese diplomatic service considered it an honor to take her to Charles. Continuing, he said, "Charles has already been notified of your arrival. He is waiting for you in the front of the Dai-Ichi building in downtown Tokyo."

Charles had been working all that day at MacArthur's headquarters. He was just finishing up his work when the phone rang. He was informed that a Lillian Kenworth had just landed and soon would arrive in front of the Dai-Ichi building. Charles couldn't believe what he was hearing and asked the person to repeat slowly what he had said. It finally soaked in, and he felt a surge of joy. He didn't bother to gather his things. He rushed to the front of the building. There he paced back and forth. He looked in the direction of the airport.

It was a beautiful fall day. Across the street was the moat that surrounded the imperial grounds. Fall colors were all over the grounds. He noticed none of this. He was only focusing on a car that had Lillian. Lillian was just as excited, but her views of Tokyo coming from the airport were of destruction. She was seeing starving Japanese women desperately searching debris for anything and children eating out of garbage cans. Being a Red Cross person, all this dismayed her. She forced herself to put all of these thoughts out of her mind. She wanted to have nothing but joy when she got to Charles. She closed her eyes and thought of her love for Charles.

Soon the car turned onto the avenue that ran by the imperial moat. The man escorting her said, "The Dai-Ichi building is just ahead." She opened her eyes and could see Charles pacing back and forth. The street was crowded, so Charles had not yet seen her vehicle. The automobile drew beside him, and Lillian jumped out and ran into his arms. At first, all they did was to cling to each other. Nothing was said, but their bodies told them how much they cared for each other. When they finally broke their embrace, Charles led her to his jeep and drove away to his apartment.

When Charles had acquired the girls' school in Yokohama, he told his staff that he would quarter there. They were to prepare an apartment that would accommodate two people. This had just been completed. As they drove through the waste of Tokyo and Yokohama, they couldn't help but talk about what they were seeing. Lillian felt she could see a job for her. Charles said not for the foreseeable future. He wanted her all to himself. No more four day passes were going to be in their future. They settled into their apartment. The next 12 hours belonged to them alone.

When they awakened, they were facing each other. They had their first real pillow talk. They had no specific things to talk about. They just lay together and talked about, what came to mind. After they got up, Charles fixed breakfast. During breakfast he told her about the language school and how it was staffed. He said, "Before I leave for work, I am going to introduce you to Akihiko and his family. They have quarters in the same building that we are in." One of the reasons for his ability to acquire such a distinguished staff was because food and shelter were part of their salaries. Actually, that was all they received. They were grateful to have it. After breakfast, they walked to Akihiko's apartment. Charles had told them to be available so that he could introduce his fiancee' to them. Akihiko was listening for them, so they didn't have to knock. Again, Lillian surprised them. She spoke perfect Japanese. Akihiko was impressed, but Ayame was delighted. She saw the possibility of having a woman friend. They chatted in Japanese for a few minutes, and Charles asked Ayame if she would show Lillian around the neighborhood and get her acquainted with what was available. Actually, very little was available. Ayame was very excited to do this. Charles left Lillian talking to Ayame. He and Akihiko went to their conference room and met with the staff. No problems had arisen. They adjourned to their own stations.

CHAPTER 12

It was now the time for Charles to face his problem of getting MacArthur's staff to let Lillian stay. He also wanted permission to marry her. Only the most senior staff was permitted to have their wives in Japan. As he drove to the Dai-Ichi building, he pondered how he could best approach this problem. He thought maybe if he did nothing then they wouldn't have to make a decision. They might just let it ride. He didn't like this idea because they would always be waiting for the next shoe to drop. He decided that the best move was to be forthcoming. He was going to talk about her language skills and her background working with the Red Cross. He was going to emphasize about the starving Japanese population and state how she could help deal with this problem. Her knowledge of Japanese culture and her perfect language skills would fit together with great synergy. He had heard that word used frequently in the conferences where he was the interpreter.

He presented all of these ideas to his superior officer, and, surprisingly, he was impressed. He said, "I will forward this request through the chain of command to see what the decision will be." He added he would recommend it to be approved. Charles would have liked to have had an immediate "Yes". He knew they would have to go through the process.

His next duty was to Company A. He was their interpreter as they continued their task of disarming the Japanese Army. That day he had to deal with a returning Japanese Colonel. This Colonel had fought on Leyte. When General Suzuki abandoned Leyte, he went into the central mountains of Leyte. With his loyal troops, he fought a guerilla action. He was successful and was one of the last holdouts in that area. He was a very angry man and contemptuous of his captors. The people, who were in charge of him, were fed up. He understood some English, but he would only converse in Japanese. Hence, the call was for Charles.

The reason why this man was tolerated was because he was a successful guerilla commander. Headquarters felt he should be interrogated to try to discover how he was able to be so successful. Charles came to the interview and bowed in the Japanese fashion. Respectfully, he asked the Colonel what his name was. Colonel Hideaki Fujimaki was surprised that a young First Lieutenant was addressing him in such a correct and cordial manner. His anger lessened. He engaged Charles in a cooperative manner. Charles said, "I wonder how it is possible for you to have such a successful guerilla action." Charles stated further that he had fought in Leyte, and he knew how hard it must have been to carry on a guerilla action in the mountains. This sympathetic approach was very pleasing to Colonel Fujimaki, so much so, that he opened up and talked about his experience as a guerilla commander. Before they had started to talk about his guerilla activities, Charles had told the Colonel that he would like to record what the Colonel had to say. The Colonel was pleased by his interest and readily agreed. By the end of his interrogation, Charles had much information. He asked the Colonel if he would stay in custody for a few days so that he could talk to him further about his guerilla experiences. The Colonel knew that he really had no choice. He appreciated this kindness. He said, "Yes." The interview ended.

The intelligence staff of the 132nd Regiment was not surprised by Charles' performance. They told him that MacArthur's intelligence group had requested information concerning Colonel Fujimaki. The information he had gotten was immediately to be brought to their attention. They asked if Charles would take it to them. He rushed to the Dai-Ichi building and was ushered into the office of the chief of intelligence. Charles saluted sharply and presented his interview. The intelligence officer asked Charles to wait outside in the waiting room. While he waited, this officer came out of his office and told Charles to stay as he had an appointment to make. Actually, he had called General MacArthur and exclaimed about Charles' interview. The General wanted to read it. MacArthur read the interview two times. He called in Colonel Gray and said, "Now that is a real interrogator." He said further, "I want to meet this interviewer at once." The officer came back to Charles and told him that General MacArthur wanted to see him. Charles entered into MacArthur's office and saluted smartly. MacArthur said, "I am impressed by your interview of Colonel Hideaki Fujimaki." He told him that he wanted him transferred to his staff immediately. MacArthur had a memory of everything that passed over his desk. He remembered that a Charles Bettendorf had requested for his fiancee' to be allowed to stay in Japan. He asked Bettendorf if he was that Lieutenant Bettendorf. He answered with a clear firm answer, "Yes, Sir." MacArthur smiled and said, "I was about to deny your request when I received your interview." He continued to say that if Charles' fiancee' was as talented as he was, then he could not afford to lose her. He was going to make an exception to his orders and allow her to remain. He turned to his intelligence officer and said, "I want you to interview this young lady and see how best we can use her." He dismissed both officers.

Charles left finding it hard to believe, what had happened. The intelligence officer told Charles his transfer orders would be issued immediately. He was to report tomorrow with Lillian. He would interview her. The day had moved fast for Charles. All he wanted to do was to get to Lillian as fast as he could. The good news was over loading his mind.

CHAPTER 13

When he arrived at their apartment, he found Lillian cooking supper. He grabbed her and lifted her off her feet. He gave her a big kiss and began telling her, what had happened (mainly, she could stay). Lillian was extremely happy. All she could think of was that they could get married. That word was big in her mind. She told Charles that she wanted to plan her wedding now! She wanted her name to be Bettendorf. Charles was excited about his job. Lillian was excited about their wedding. As things settled down, Charles told the rest of what happened.

He related about his interview with MacArthur. He said that both of them were to go to Colonel Gray's office so that she could be interviewed. They wanted to find out how she could be used by the intelligence service. Lillian was frightened by this. She asked Charles how she was supposed to prepare for this interview. Charles said, "Just be you." They stopped and caught their breath. Smiling at each other, Charles winked at her and said, "I am tired and I think that we should lie down for a while." Lillian winked back. They had a late supper. They both dreamed that night. Each dreamed what they most wished for.

The next morning they left for their appointment. They arrived early and sat waiting for Colonel Gray. On his arrival, they went immediately into his office. Bettendorf introduced Lillian. He was instantly proud of how gracious she was in addressing the Colonel. The Colonel was impressed by her responses. But, most of all, he was impressed by her beauty. What he saw was a young, moderately tall, well formed, young lady. She was blond headed with a reddish tinge to her hair. Her eyes were a deep dark blue, and she had the cutest turned up nose. He suddenly said to himself, "Stop these thoughts." He told himself to get down to business. This change of orientation was covered by his being gruff for a few minutes. Lillian realized, what was happening, and felt in control of the interview.

She immediately launched into describing her qualifications. She told him she felt she was qualified to be an interpreter of Japanese and Tagalog languages. She wanted to emphasize her administrative skills. She pointed out that one of their biggest problems was feeding the starving Japanese people. Her Red Cross experience made her very qualified in this area. In other words, when she got through with the interview, Colonel Gray wondered how they ever got along without her. It was a two hour interview. Charles was tremendously proud of her.

Soon after they left, Colonel Gray went to MacArthur's morning conference. At the end of the conference, he asked Colonel Gray if he had interviewed Bettendorf's fiancee'. He replied that he was very impressed with her. He said, "She spoke well and presented many fresh ideas of how to address the problems of a starving Japanese population." He said, "I am not qualified to evaluate her language skills. I called the Japanese diplomatic personnel that met her when she arrived in Japan. I talked with the person, who brought her to the Dai-Ichi building. He found she was well schooled in Japanese culture and language. He said, "We talked in Japanese all the way to our destination." The diplomat felt like he was talking to a colleague. I assumed that this meant that she really knew the Japanese language." He continued saying that he thought this couple had much to offer his staff. MacArthur was pleased and said, "Get them involved."

Since Lillian and Charles had no immediate duties, they went outside and started walking. They thought the street name said Yaraku-Cho.

They weren't sure, but they both were impressed with the moat and the imperial grounds. Lillian told Charles it was such a pretty day that they should go across the moat bridge and visit the imperial grounds. It was a good idea, so off they went. Lillian had been in Japanese gardens before, and she told Charles that the grounds were like a large Japanese Garden. They went past the partially destroyed imperial palace. There were some other buildings, but they had no idea, what they were.

They were supposed to be in Colonel Gray's office by 1400. It was a short time after their arrival that they saw the Colonel. It was a pleasant exchange. He informed them that for the time being, Lillian would be an interpreter. Her ideas about food distribution for the starving Japanese people were still being studied. He said, "Charles, you are to continue with your language school, and you are to be the main interpreter for General MacArthur." They were dismissed and went back to their apartment.

For the next few weeks they were involved in routine matters. Charles finished his interviewing of Colonel Hideaki Fujimari. They didn't become friends, but they respected each other. Charles told him that conditions were severe in Japan, and if any time in the future he could be of help, he would be available. Hideaki didn't want to be indebted to Charles. He thanked him, and said he had resources. He also said that he must find his wife and his children. Hideaki turned and left the stockade.

It was Sunday morning and Lillian and Charles were relaxing when one of the servants of the school said a woman was at the gate of the school. She wanted to speak with Lillian. The servant said her name was Aiko Yamamoto. Lillian jumped up and ran to the gate. There stood Aiko with her two girls. They looked half starved. Aiko looked ashamed. There were tears in her eyes. Lillian brought her to their apartment. When they sat down, she immediately served tea and cakes. She could see that they were starving. Aiko and the girls tried not to show how hungry they were. They ate the cakes very slowly. Aiko could carry on the facade no longer and burst out crying. Lillian held her in her arms and tried to console her. Slowly, her story came out. She said, "Both of my families are starving. There is no heat in their homes. I have only the clothes I wore when I came to Japan." Continuing she said, "I cannot stand it any longer seeing my daughters crying for food during the night." She said, "Lillian, you are my only hope for surviving." Lillian asked about Isabella. Aiko said, "I took her to the Filipino embassy, and they sent her home." Charles listened, and as they talked, he went into the kitchen and started cooking. He cooked a large bowl of rice and put left over fish in the rice. That Saturday, they had gotten some milk, and he filled three glasses full to the brim. While they were talking, he brought out the food and put it before them. The gratitude and relief in their eyes was heart rendering.

Lillian and Charles left the room so they could eat alone. He warned them to eat slowly as they were starved. He and Lillian went into the outside hall and talked about what they could do about their situation. At the moment, all Lillian could think of was keeping them safe. Charles felt that Aiko needed a job and a place to stay. He said, "I have no female teachers on my staff and all of our students are males." He thought that all they were teaching now was language and nothing of Japanese culture. He said, "Maybe I ought to start a course on Japanese culture and etiquette." Lillian immediately thought that this was a good idea. She reminded Charles that it was his understanding of Japanese military etiquette, that enabled him to get such a great interview with Hideaki. This interview enabled them to be together.

Charles called Akihiko to come to his apartment. He took him into another room and told him of his intention to start a new class on Japanese culture and etiquette. Akihiko asked, "Who will teach this course?" Charles told him about Aiko Yamamoto. While he was talking to Akihiko, Lillian explained to Aiko the idea of having a teaching job at the language institute. She said, "You would have no salary, but you would have food and shelter." It was impossible to describe her joy and relief. Now she could feed her children and have a safe, warm place to live. Charles and Lillian spent the rest of the day getting Aiko set up in her apartment.

When Akihiko told Ayame about Aiko Yamamoto, she asked, "What was her maiden name?" Akihiko said he thought that it was Suzuki. Ayame exclaimed, "I know Aiko! We were in school together." She told Akihiko what an important family Aiko came from. She got up and immediately went to Lillian's apartment and asked to speak to Aiko. Aiko immediately recognized her. They were excited to be reunited. Ayame said, "Now we have three women friends." Lillian interrupted and said, "I have a matron of honor and one bridesmaid. Charles, it is time for us to get married."

She had been wondering how she was going to get a marriage license. She asked the two women if they had had marriage licenses. It seemed they had something similar to a marriage license. Lillian commissioned them to find out about this. Lillian's mind was in a whirl. She must write her parents about her coming marriage to Charles. She and Charles had not talked about her family since the first days of their being together. She remembered them talking about their parents and how Charles had an unloving family. Now, she felt she must present her family to Charles in detail. For example, Charles did not know that she had four brothers and one sister. She must tell him more since they were going to get married. Charles had wanted this marriage for a long time.

All of the efforts of Ayame and Aiko to get a marriage license for Charles and Lillian were to no avail. The Japanese government was not working. It was the 15th of November, 1945, and Japan would not have a constitution until July, 1946. Lillian felt her only hope was to have her parents get a marriage license in Georgia. She had written her family about her feelings for Charles and said they wanted to get married. Her parents felt it was better to listen and not respond to her concerning their feelings about their relationship. When they got her request for a marriage license, they knew they had to say what they had been discussing.

Their return letter to Lillian said they felt that she and Charles were too young to marry. She was 21 and Charles was 20. It would be better if they waited and let their relationship mature. Lillian replied with some anger. She said, "Charles is 20, but let me remind you what he has accomplished in the past year. First, he fought off single-handedly Japanese paratroopers, who were attacking his aid station. It just so happened, he saved my life. He did a dangerous patrol around Ormoc that led to the capture of that city. In the battles in southern Luzon, he received a Bronze and a Silver Star. He mastered the Japanese language and now he is the official interpreter for General MacArthur. He has organized a language school teaching the Japanese language to United States Army personnel. He may be 20 years old chronologically, but to me, he is a mature man. For myself, I have had more maturing experiences than most women of 40. Besides all of this, Charles and I have exchanged personal vows of marriage. It is my hope that with this information, you will help us get a marriage license." She signed it "Your loving daughter, Lillian." The answer to this letter was a marriage license with the two words, "Good luck".

By this time, it was December 15, 1945. Lillian was glad to get the license but disturbed by their limited response. She immediately made plans for their wedding. An Army Chaplain would administer the vows. Aiko would be her matron of honor and Akemi would be her flower girl. Charles' best man would be Captain Petrie and his second, Master Sergeant Jones. It was a quiet marriage that satisfied both of them. Ayame and Aiko produced a great Japanese wedding feast.

All through this trying time, both Charles and Lillian had continued in their interpreting work. The school was advancing well. Aiko had developed her program and her two girls and Ayame's two girls began to have a more normal life. Akemi, Asami, Chie, and Chiase were constantly together. The staff of the school called them the "A.C. Girls". They would carry this name with them every time they were together.

It was in early January that ex-Colonel Hideaki Fujimaki appeared at the gate of the language school. He requested to speak with Lieutenant Bettendorf. The person at the gate reported, "We have no Lieutenant Bettendorf here. There is a Captain Bettendorf." Ex-Colonel Fujimaki smiled to himself and thought, so you got a promotion. He said, "May I have an appointment with him?" The gate keeper went to Captain Bettendorf and said, "A shabby Japanese man is at the gate claiming to be a Colonel Fujimaki. He is requesting a meeting with you." Charles jumped and went to the gate. He gave a smart salute to Fujimaki, and he returned it. Fujimaki was grateful for the way that Charles greeted him. By looking at Fujimaki, Charles could see he was in a desperate condition. Charles took him to his apartment instead of his office. He said, "We are having a late breakfast. We would be honored if Colonel Fujimaki would join my wife and me for breakfast." Fujimaki turned to Lillian and bowed deeply. She returned with a bow talking to him in Japanese. All of this kindness was overwhelming to Fujimaki. He almost collapsed. Charles grabbed him and led him to a chair. Lillian rushed into the kitchen and got him a glass of milk. He drank if hungrily. He then began to tell them, what had happened to him over the past two months.

When he left Charles, he went in search of his wife and his children. His search ended quickly, for when he came to their house, he found nothing but ashes. He found a neighbor that knew his family and was told they were incinerated in the Tokyo fire storm. He reported that some ashes were found, but they were not kept. His despair overwhelmed him, and he just wandered around lost. He went to his army headquarters for help. Even though he was considered an officer, who had been honorable, and had not surrendered until the Emperor ordered, they could do nothing to help him. Nothing was available for him. He found himself wandering around Tokyo in his tropical Japanese uniform. He said, "I ate out of garbage cans and slept wherever I could." It took all this time before he could force himself to come to Charles, an ex-enemy, and ask for help. He said, "I want a job so I can take care of myself." Charles said, "Let's stop talking and go to breakfast."

It was Fujimaki's first meal he had eaten since leaving the stockade. It was the second breakfast for Charles and Lillian. After they had eaten, Charles said, "I have been looking for a security chief. His responsibility would be to keep the facility secure and to supervise the maintenance of the facility. Would you be interested in this position?" Fujimaki arose and stood erect and said, "I would be honored to accept this position." He continued in a formal way and said, "Honorable Captain, would food, quarters, and uniforms go with the position?" Charles said, "Yes, that is the salary of the position." Charles said, "I have no money available to offer you." Fujimaki was pleased with the conditions. While all of this discussion was going on, Hideaki was thinking, "He is open with me and I need to be open with him." He said, "Captain Bettendorf, I need to be honest and open with you. You need to know what kind of a person I am. I have always wanted to be in the Army. I went to the Japanese military academy, and I was a cruel officer to my men and, especially to American prisoners. Many times I killed enemy soldiers when I found them wounded. I would take no prisoners. I look at myself now as an evil person, an animal. I have lost everything. Prior to now, the only persons I loved were my wife and my children. Your helping me when I am helpless is troubling to me. How can I repay you?" Charles said, "You owe me only a honest day's work." He took him to meet all of the staff. His position and duties were explained, and he was taken to his room in the bachelor's quarters. There was a bed and warm clothes. Charles said, "Your duties will start tomorrow, and at the time, I will introduce you to the two men you will supervise." When he left, Fujimaki said to himself, "How was it possible that I could have met such an honorable man?" His thoughts continued with his wondering how could such a man come about. He had heard that most of the American soldiers were Christians. He practiced Shintoism and Buddhism. He wondered if he should investigate Christianity.

Lillian had not heard from her parents since receiving the license. She had written a thank you note, but no reply. It troubled her, but she was not going to let it affect her happiness. In the middle of January, 1946, she received a letter from them. She could remember the exact date because on January 16, 1946, the 132nd infantry regiment was decommissioned, and Charles' best friends, Captain Petrie and Master Sergeant Jones left for home.

Before they left, they sat down with Charles and had long talks. They wanted their relationships to continue when they got back to the States. Sam Petrie said, "We have not told each other about our lives before the war." He said the following: He was born in 1912, and went to Louisiana State University. He was in the Infantry Cadet Corp and graduated in 1934 at age 22. He left school and returned to his home in Nacogdoches, Texas. In that year, he married, and his baby boy was born. In the latter part of 1934, he joined his father-in-law's insurance firm. He had just become proficient in this business when in 1936, his father-in-law died. He and his wife, Mary, took over the business. For the next five years, the business slowly grew. As were so many others, they were handicapped by the depression. 1940 and 1941 were the best years of their business life. He had joined the Texas National Guard -- 132nd Infantry Regiment -- in 1939. In 1941, they had a baby girl. When war was declared, he was called up and commissioned a 2nd Lieutenant. His wife took over the business, and over the next five years, she ran it well. Now he was going home to Nacogdoches, Texas, to a company his wife had developed. He would be with a wife, who he had been married to for twelve years but only lived with for seven years. He would have a twelve year old son and a six year old daughter that he had not seen for five years. He stopped and was silent for a few minutes. He continued and said, "I was thinking I was going home to a woman, who had spent five years away from me. All we both know about the other is through letters. Physically, we are strangers. I am wondering how we will feel when we start our sexual life together. I fear we will be strangers having sex and pretending that we have reestablished ourselves when so much has happened to us that we could never share it with each other. How can I tell her about how it was killing and threatened with being killed? How can she share with me the lonely nights with sick children, and the days she worried if she could make it in the business? As I think of all of this, I am wondering if maybe I should just stay here. Then, the memory of the warm loving wife I left comes over me. I know I can make it." Charles and David were deeply touched by what he had said.

David Jones thought that Sam had expressed well the same fears that oppressed him. Sergeant David Jones started telling his story. He was born in 1908. He was too young to fight in World War One. He wanted to be in the regular Army. When he was eighteen, he did join the Army. He said, "I was involved in the expelling of the World War One veterans in their march on Washington, D.C. They were demanding the bonuses that they had been promised. He disliked, what had happened. He said MacArthur ordered the assault on the veterans. He didn't reenlist in 1935 because of this. It was a foolish decision on his part as there was no work available. He hoboed for two years and ended up in a small west Texas town called Lamesa. He was bumming around and heard of a nearby ranch that was hiring. When he got to the ranch, he found that it was run by a young lady. Apparently, she was doing poorly, and all she could offer was room and board. No one had taken this offer, but he was hungry. He told her he would work for a while.

As it turned out, he worked there for four years and married her in the second year he was there. Mildred, to him, was a beautiful young lady. It became obvious to him that several ranchers were trying to make Mildred fail. This angered him, and he told his boss, Mildred, that he would work for her until she had a secure ranch. Mildred told him how much his promise meant to her. Over the next few months, he vigorously defended her cattle and her property. The ranchers soon realized that Mildred was going to be successful and stopped harassing her. When the two years was up, Jones knew he was in love with Mildred. He saw himself as being a man without any assets. He felt his chance to marry Mildred was next to zero. It hurt him to be around her. One day he couldn't stand it any longer and came to Mildred and said, "I am leaving." She said, "Why are you leaving when you know how much I need you?" He replied, "Mildred, I am just a tramp that happened to find you. I have fallen in love with you. I know you had no idea that this was happening, and I can't stay here feeling this way." She told me I was a fool to think that she could never love me. She said, "I knew that I was in love with you when you stood up so strongly for me against my greedy neighbors." He could hardly believe what he had heard, but his body did. He ran to her and held her close. They clung together. He continued, "That started the happiest years of my life. We fit well together and in three years, we had two boys. When the Japs hit Pearl Harbor, I immediately enlisted and was first assigned to a recruiting station in Lubbock, Texas. I volunteered for infantry duty and was eventually sent to the 132nd infantry regiment. I last saw my wife and my two boys in early 1942. I left when my boys were two and one. Now, they are seven and six."

Both men felt strange going home. Sam had a company, and David had a ranch to take care of. They ended their talks with Charles' story and made a commitment to get together annually when Charles returned home. They were able to do this for a while and then lost contact with each other.

It was a happy and sad day for Lillian. In the letter, her parents said they were coming to Japan to see them. They should arrive on or about February first. She was shocked but pleased. She hoped that this visit would bring them back together.

That night she told Charles about their coming. She told him from the very first, they had felt they were too young to marry. He said, "They will see how mature we are and how happy we are. It surely should assure them that we have a successful marriage."

Fujimaki was an immediate success. There had been some problems with thieves. This behavior stopped immediately. The grounds were spotless. All of the staff had lunch together. This was a requirement of Charles as he wanted them to function as a family. One day Fujimaki was sitting next to Aiko. They struck up a conversation. During that conversation, he found out that her deceased husband had been a Captain in the Japanese Navy and was killed defending Manila. He found out about, what had happened to her and her two girls. She inquired about his family, and all he would say was that they were dead. He abruptly got up and left. This puzzled Aiko.

Charles continued his work with the intelligence staff. He was exposed to all of their discussions concerning the new constitution for the Japanese people. Some wanted to remove the emperor, but MacArthur wanted to retain him as a figurehead. He felt it would help get the support of the people. It was obvious that his ideas would prevail.

The group representing the allies tried to influence this process. There was one incident when Russia tried to usurp the group, but this was stopped. Russia wanted Japan to be a communistic nation, and Britain and Australia wanted Japan to be a social democracy with the abolishment of the emperor. The British and Australians felt that the emperor was instrumental in many of the decisions made in the war. They felt that he approved the bombing of Pearl Harbor and the attack on the British colonies as well as the Dutch. These accusations were later proved true, but MacArthur overruled them. The one idea that Australia prevailed on was how they were to treat labor unions. Australia was ruled by a labor party, hence, their interest in labor unions.

Lillian continued her interpreting work. The supply of food improved. There was more available for the populace. MacArthur's staff started to talk to her about her ideas of how to distribute food to the starving people. It would be well into 1946 before her ideas were implemented.

CHAPTER 14

February one finally came. Lillian had received a telegram from her parents that they were leaving San Francisco at 2400 hours on January 31st. They said they would lose a day. She could figure the approximate time they would arrive at the Tokyo airport. They were flying Northwestern Airlines, Flight 410. She and Charles were waiting. When they got off the plane, they immediately saw Lillian. They rushed towards her and hugged her. Both were talking and expressing their joy of being with her at last. She had been gone for two years. When the excitement lessened, Lillian introduced Charles. To Lillian's mother's eyes, she was impressed by how handsome he was. Her father noticed that he was a Captain and how erect he was. He noticed his combat infantry badge and the Bronze and Silver Stars. Needless to say, he was impressed. Charles knew that he was not to salute a civilian, but he knew his father-in-law was a retired, disabled, regular Army officer. He felt he deserved a salute. So, he hugged his mother-in-law and saluted his father-in-law. These actions impressed them, and it seemed that they had gotten off on the right foot. The trip to Yokohama was somewhat better, but there was still much destruction. Charles had the guest rooms available, and they left her parents alone. They were very tired and needed sleep. They had flown to Anchorage, Alaska, and from there a long flight to Tokyo. They were exhausted, but they had to talk about their daughter's husband. They realized how wrong their ideas were about him. They agreed that he was the most mature 20-year old they had ever met. The mother could easily see why

Lillian was so impressed with Charles. To her, he was a very handsome man and, obviously, well educated. To her father, he couldn't understand how he could accomplish so much in the military. Lillian had said he was inducted in the Army on April 11, 1944. It was less than two years, and he was a Captain with all of those decorations. With that, they went to sleep and continued their thoughts in their dreams.

When Dan and Lucy Kenworth awakened, it took several minutes to orient themselves. They got out of bed, and Dan looked at his watch. He had reset it to Japanese time. It was six p.m. They freshened up and went to Lillian's apartment. Lillian had everything ready for dinner. All she had to do was to put it on the table. When they sat down, Lillian revealed something to Charles. She asked her father to say grace. Lillian and Charles had never discussed religion. Charles knew that Lillian was a firm Christian in her beliefs. Charles had no religion, but he respected Lillian's beliefs. When Lillian's parents arrived, so did Lillian's awareness of her faith. She decided that she would introduce it in her new family by asking her father to say grace. Charles didn't recognize the significance of this request, but he would later. During dinner they had casual talk as both remembered their letters. Charles told them about his work, but every time he started, he would unintentionally start talking about Lillian's work. Her parents noticed this and began to recognize how much Charles loved Lillian and how much he was proud of her. To some extent, Lillian did the same. When the meal was over, there was one thing that was abundantly clear. Lillian and Charles were firmly bound to each other.

After dinner, Dan started talking to Charles about his military experience. It was clear from the beginning Charles had no interest in talking about his battle experiences. Dan recognized this and only inquired about his current experiences. Charles told about an interesting event that had occurred at MacArthur's headquarters that day. On January 1, 1946, the Emperor had declared that the Japanese were to no longer consider him a deity. He firmly renounced his deity. That day he had come to MacArthur with a request that Japan be declared a Christian nation. Charles didn't know how this was going to turn out, but he found it interesting. Charles shifted the conversation to Dan and his family. Charles wanted to know about how Lillian had grown up and how she related to her brothers and sister. Dan said, "Lillian was our third child. Two of her brothers are older with two brothers and a sister being younger. The two older brothers consider her as their baby sister. The younger brothers and sister consider her a second mother." He continued, "These roles didn't seem to confuse her." He further stated the older brothers always seemed to feel that they needed to protect Lillian while the younger children felt she would protect them.

Charles, as he listened to Dan, thought that now was good time to find out what his in laws thought about their marriage. In the pause of their conversation, Charles said, "As you were talking about her older brothers being protective, I was wondering how they reacted to Lillian's marriage." Dan was a little uneasy about how the conversation was going. He decided he might as well get it into the open. He felt talking about the brothers' reaction would be easier than talking about his and Lucy's. He said, "To begin with, they were concerned and almost angry. They felt that you had taken advantage of Lillian's gratitude for your saving her life. Her letters about how you conducted yourself in combat impressed them. Both of them were in Europe with Patton's Third Army and were in many battles. They knew how dangerous your combat must have been in order for you to get the Bronze and Silver Stars. Their whole attitude changed. They started bragging about their baby sister being engaged to a real soldier." He continued, "Now, they think Lillian made a great decision in marrying you and want you to consider them as brothers." He went further and said, "They would have come to Japan if they could have afforded it. They were discharged from the Army in October, 1945, and are back in college under the G.I. Bill. Bill, the oldest, was studying law, and Joe was studying business. Neither wanted the military as a career."

Lillian and her mother joined them at this point, and the conversation went in other directions.

That night when Lillian and Charles were pillow talking, he told her about their conversation. For the time being, there was no more talk about their marriage.

The next few weeks were filled with activities connected with Lillian's and Charles' work. Lucy would be with Lillian, and Dan would be with Charles. Dan's being with Charles brought him in contact with some old military friends. This was exciting for Dan as he had missed his military experiences. Late in the day, he and his old friends would meet in the senior officers' club and reminisce about times gone by. It was during one of these times that Dan asked how Charles was doing as a military officer. His friends paused as if they were reluctant to tell the truth. Dan felt very uncomfortable and wished he had not brought up the subject. When they saw him squirm, they burst out laughing. Dan wasn't amused and was a bit angry. They immediately said they were just joking with him. They knew that he was concerned about his daughter's recent marriage. With that over, they told him what they thought of Charles. First they said, "He is a fine battle tested officer. He has ability for strategic planning. His tactical ability expressed itself by the two actions that led to his two medals." They continued by relating the excellent work he was doing in the intelligence department. They didn't think much of his language school, but MacArthur was all for it. Dan was amazed by what he had heard. That evening as he was driving home with Charles, he found himself looking at Charles. He was trying on his growing image of Charles. One thing was clear to him: He had a growing proud for him. He was seeing their marriage in a different light.

Lucy was having the same type of experience with Lillian. She was discovering that the young girl, who had left home, was no longer a girl, but a capable woman, who dealt with complex problems in a calm and effective manner. That night when Dan and Lucy were alone, they shared their new awareness. Dan said that he, not only admired the guy, but also liked him. Lucy was ahead of him in regards to Charles. She loved him as if he were one of her boys. She said she no longer felt that Lillian had been taken advantage of. She now felt that Lillian saw a good thing and took advantage of it. She ended by saying, "Lillian is one smart gal." Dan was impressed by her strong feelings, and he went to sleep with many changing thoughts. From then on, whole attitudes changed in how they related to their children. Charles and Lillian were aware of the change and were very grateful. It was much later before they found out, what had happened.

Dan and Lucy had expected to stay for one month, but they were having so much fun they decided to stay a second month. They wanted to see more of Japan. They were interested in the Shinto religion and wanted to visit some of the Shinto shrines. Charles had studied about the Shinto religion and knew where the significant shrines were. They went to the Heian Jingu Shrine in Kyoto. He told them that it was dedicated to Emperor Kammu and Emperor Komei. They had wanted to go to the Itsukushima Shrine. It was located in the Hiroshima Prefecture. This area was still too radioactive. Charles told them that it was one of the treasures of Japan.

In Kyoto they wanted to go into the Heian Jingu Shrine. Charles instructed them in the rituals used to enter this shrine. He said, "You approach the entrance and bow respectfully. If there is a hand washing basin provided, then you perform Temizu. This means that you wash your left hand first, then your right hand. Then you rinse your mouth, and if your feet need it, you wash your feet. After that you tip the ladle backwards to wash the ladle handle with the remaining water. The ladle is then placed face down on the rack where you found it." Charles continued by saying, "If a bell is there, you could ring it prior to prayers. If there is a box for donations, a modest donation is required." He said, "Normally, there is a sequence of bows and claps as you pray. As you finish your last prayer, you hold your hands together from the last clap. You place your clasped hands in front of your heart for a closing bow." They all did their best to perform. Lillian and Charles had attended Aiko's culture classes and did well.

There were many other activities, but the one that they all remembered was the trip to Mt. Fuji. They stayed in a quaint little inn. The walls were decorated paper, as were the doors. They slept on pads on the floor. They ate sitting on cushions on the floor around a hibashi with a bowl of rice in the center of the hibashi. Separate dishes were brought in as needed, and they struggled with chop sticks. All of this took place in the evening after their climb up Mt. Fuji. Actually, they got only to the 10,000 foot level. There were cute little way stations on the way up. They stopped and admired the scenery.

The second month ended too soon. When they were saying goodbye at the airport, Lucy and Dan kissed them both and said that they loved them. As they left the airport, they both knew that they were back in the family.

CHAPTER 15

Many other things were happening. To Charles the most significant was Hideaki. Hideaki came to him and said, "I need to talk to you." Charles knew that something was bothering him for he seemed preoccupied. He started talking about, what had happened to him, when he heard the Emperor's taped message of defeat. He was in a mountain hideout. He had not been able to escape with General Suzuki, and had retreated into the remote jungles of Leyte. The squeaky voice of the Emperor bothered him, and he was even more disturbed when the Emperor, on January 1st, said that he was no longer a deity. He continued saying, "I began thinking about all I had lost in the name of my duty to the Emperor. I had lost my wife, my children, and my country. I have memories of all of the cruel things I did to American prisoners. Then I met you. You had been my enemy, yet when I was in great need, you literally saved my life. You gave me the possibility of a new and better life. All of my life, I have practiced my Shinto and Buddhist religions. These religions taught me to be respectful of my ancestors and to worship and obey my Emperor even if it caused my death. Now, I find my Emperor is a squeaky small man, who is more interested in building an empire than taking care of his people. I can no longer believe in my religion or my government. I need to talk to someone, and you are my only true friend." Charles knew that Hideaki respected him but not that he considered him as a best friend.

Charles answered saying, "The Japanese government is developing a new constitution. I particularly like the women suffrage." He said, "Ayame and Aiko are smart women, and they can contribute much to their new country by being able to participate in its governing." Hideaki became impatient with Charles and said, "I don't give a dam about government. What concerns me is - What do I believe in?" Charles thought he was leading him into religion, and he had no religion. Before he could say anything else, Hideaki said, "You are a kind and forgiving person. I want to be that way. I want to know more about your Christian religion." Charles said, "I am not religious. I believe in Jesus' ministry of love, but the idea of a personal God is beyond me. I have seen too many deaths and cruelty to believe in a personal God. Lillian is a dedicated Christian, and she can teach you about Christianity." They talked about other things, and Hideaki said, "I will talk to Lillian."

CHAPTER 16

When Hideaki left, Charles started to think about his religious feelings. He realized that he had never thought seriously about religion. He had just dumped it into a theological garbage can. He wondered why he had done this. His first thought was of his experiences in the jungles of Queensland, Australia. He was in his fifth week of O.C.S. training. They were doing patrol exercises involved in jungle fighting. He was the right shoulder of a diamond patrol formation. This put him about 20 feet from the jungle trail they were following. As they advanced, he found that he had lost contact with his patrol. He was lost in no man's land. No man's land was about ten miles north of Port Douglas. He immediately began to consider what he must do. He first considered calling out to the members of his patrol. He felt that if he did, he would have defeated the purpose of the patrol. His only solution was to find his way back to their forward base. This was a problem as the jungle was so dense he could not see the sun clearly. He remembered that his base was on the banks of a large river. He was in the basin that drained to this river. He decided to find a stream and follow it to the river. When he got to the river, he had to decide which direction he would go. He started remembering the direction that the patrol had taken on leaving their station. They had headed due east. He was south of the trail when he got lost. Since he must have been facing east when he got lost, he thought that he must have gone south. The stream he found flowed west. The river flowed in a north-south direction. This must mean that he was downstream from his station. He started up stream, and in three hours, he was back at his base. They were just preparing a search team for him when he walked in. They were very surprised that he had found his way back to the base as they had lost candidates on this exercise and never found them. He said, "Why does this memory come to my mind?" I was asking questions about religion. It was then that he remembered that while he was lost, he never prayed for God's help. It was the first time he had begun to think about a personal God. As he continued with his war experiences, he became convinced that there was no personal God. No personal God would permit such pain, death, and destruction of human lives.

This was only part of the answer. He would have to look deeper. The next thought was describing his experiences from the ages of seven to thirteen. He was living in El Dorado, Arkansas. His father was driving him to the First Methodist Church. He was going to Sunday school. His father and mother never went to church, but he and his sister were required to go to Sunday school every Sunday. He remembered being taught the Bible, and about how sinful he was. He didn't know, what sin was, but he was terrified that he must be covered with it. Everything he did raised a question of whether he was sinful. In the summer, he was exposed to revivals. There, sin was all they talked about. When he started having erections, he knew for sure that he was very sinful. He started having nightmares. They were connected with his erections. It wasn't until he was in high school that he realized that all of this fear was nonsense. He should be proud that he was sexually able.

Why did it take so long for him to discover this? He immediately realized that he could never talk with his parents about his problems. His mother always pleaded helplessness, and his dad wasn't interested in talking with him. He felt that his religious teachings had caused him pain and robbed him of having a normal childhood. He realized this was not the complete story of his aversion to religion, but it stimulated him to explore further.

In college he took religious courses. He studied the Bible, and he sought out different religions. All emphasized sin. They complicated it further by their dogmas. He could not grasp the Trinity, the ascension of Christ, and he never found comfort in prayer. The only prayer that he remembered was the Lord's Prayer. On many occasions when he felt despair, he did use the Lord's Prayer. This prayer was to a personal God. He rarely gained any comfort from it. He finally decided that he would have to depend on himself and not have a personal God.

He realized that Hideaki needed a God and longed for one. He didn't have this longing, and felt that he must depend on himself. As his thoughts on this subject ended, he said to himself, "I must not have the God genes that would give me a longing for a personal God."

Lillian, too, had important things to catch up on. The one that concerned her was Aiko. Aiko had come to her in tears. She said that she and Hideaki were seeing each other, and, suddenly, he had stopped seeing her. Lillian had been teaching Hideaki about Christianity, and he had talked about his feelings for Aiko. He said, "I am falling in love with Aiko." It wouldn't work out with his having so much anger over the loss of his first wife. When Aiko wanted to talk about their loss, he had to leave. It just stirred up too much anger. So, he stayed away from her. Lillian made no comment and just continued their lessons.

As they progressed, she felt that he needed contact with Japanese Christians. She knew they had suffered and were repressed by the war government. There was one Christian group that had survived this repression and expressed courage. She knew Hideaki would respect them. The group was the Todaisha Missionary Group. She found out where they met and convinced Hideaki to go there. His second meeting was to be that very day, that she and Aiko were talking about Aiko's feelings for Hideaki. Lillian wouldn't tell Aiko of her meetings with

Hideaki, but she did tell her of this meeting that she knew he would attend. She encouraged Aiko to go and see what would happen.

Aiko did go to the Todaisha meeting. Hideaki was surprised to see her there. Aiko sat next to Hideaki so that he would have to recognize her. After the services, meetings were held for people that wanted to know more about the Christian religion. Both were in this group. That day, the subject was forgiveness. This was very important to Hideaki. Each participant was expected to talk about their need for forgiveness.

Hideaki rose and said, "I am very angry about the loss of my wife and children. I was a Colonel in the Japanese Army, and I was a cruel commander. I was ruthless with my troops and brutal with my prisoners of war. I believed in the deity of my Emperor. I would die for him. Now I feel betrayed by my government. I am no longer a follower of Shinto. My closest friend is an American infantry officer. We probably fought against each other in Leyte. After the war, I was returned to Japan. I met this man while I was being demilitarized. Later he helped me when I was starving. He gave me a job, and his kindness brought the possibility of love into my life. I asked him to help me to find out about Christianity as I felt that he was influenced by it. His wife helped me to understand Christianity, but I couldn't get rid of my anger. I could not forgive. This was causing me much distress. This woman sitting beside me is a person that I love very much, but I fear that my anger and unforgiveness will destroy our relationship. I withdrew from her saying nothing to her. I know I have hurt her. It was a great surprise to me for her to be here as I could find no way to reunite with her." He sat down and looked straight forward fearing to look at Aiko.

The leader rose and said, "Let us all pray for Brother Hideaki." The prayer was long and very moving. During the prayer, Aiko reached for Hideaki's hand and held it firmly. When the prayer was over, the leader said, "Let us all hug Brother Hideaki and tell him that our love, and the love of Christ will relieve him of his anger and give him power to forgive." The first one to hug him was Aiko. She included a gentle kiss. Hideaki was deeply moved. He couldn't let go of Aiko. No miracle happened to Hideaki that evening, but the love of Aiko resolved him to give up his anger.

Over the next two months their relationship grew. Aiko's two daughters were accepting him as a father. He rejoiced in this as he had a family again. They had a simple Christian wedding, and he moved into Aiko's apartment. There were now three families living in the language school. They were very close to each other and would be friends the rest of their lives.

It was approaching May, 1946. A new person was coming into Charles' life. All during the time that he had worked in MacArthur's headquarters, he had been in contact with the Japanese foreign ministry. When MacArthur appointed Shigeru Yoshida as foreign minister, Charles was very pleased. He had several conversations with Yoshida. On May 1, 1946, Yoshida was appointed Prime Minister of Japan. This move would allow Japan to start recovering its economy. As Japan recovered, it was obvious to Charles that he would be leaving Japan within the next year. The approval of the constitution in July, 1946, made it possible for Japan to be a recovering sovereign nation.

Charles and Lillian continued to grow in their relationship. They were getting hints that Charles might be released from his five year commitment in the not too distant future. Charles applied to his old college, Vanderbilt University, with the idea of taking courses by mail. He needed one year of pre-med studies to be eligible to enter medical school.

His old teacher of German, Professor Mayfield, replied to his inquiry. He stated if he took the required courses at Tokyo University, then

Vanderbilt would accept their credits. If the grades were acceptable, then he would help Charles get accepted in Vanderbilt Medical School.

Charles found out what courses that were required and enrolled in Tokyo University. Akihiko had already left the language school and was teaching in his old department of languages. He and Ayame were still living at the language school, but they had found an apartment and were moving out the next week. Three families were beginning to go their own paths. Akihiko helped Charles matriculate.

When Akihiko left the language school, he felt like he had lost his family. He wondered why he should feel this way. This brought back memories of his childhood. His parents were farmers. They rented five acres of land and were constantly working. He was the eldest child of eight children. As soon as he could, he was working with his father. His father was a quiet man, who demanded as much of himself as he demanded of his children. From an early age, his father realized that Akihiko was different from the other children. He seemed to want to read all of the time. He did his share of the work, but in his quiet moments, he would be reading. He excelled in school. Eventually, he was awarded a military scholarship to Tokyo Imperial University. His parents never talked with each other. The children were taught to be quiet and work hard. There was no joy in his family. Life was grim, and they were grim. When he went to the university, he had no money and almost starved before he was brought into Ayame's family. Professor Kichiro Yasada, Ayame's father, was head of the department of languages. He admired Akihiko and made him a part of the family. He slowly abandoned his quiet ways and moved away from his cold unfeeling self. This change attracted Ayame, and they began to date. They married and for the first time, he felt alive.

He was 25 years old in 1934. At that time, Japan was controlled by a militaristic government. Many citizens were being drafted into the Army. The Army inducted Akihiko. They were forming a special group of men, who spoke fluently in the language of the country they were planning to attack. Akihiko spoke fluent English. Even as early as 1934, Japan was preparing for war with the United States. The induction into the Army was like going back to the farm. He was told not to talk, but work. He regressed from his open happy self to a stern, emotionless automaton. When he would return home to Ayame, it would take weeks for him to become warm again. He could never get all the way there as he had to return to his unit.

From 1934 to 1941, life was like this. During those years Chiase and Chie would know him as a stern father. Only Ayame knew him to be a loving man. When the war started, the Army attached him to the 48th infantry division, and they left to invade the Philippines. He felt the same loss that he was experiencing now as he was leaving the language school. He felt that Charles had rescued him from the Japanese Army, restored his family to him, and given him a chance to know that there was a kind and giving person in this world like his father-in-law.

A few weeks later, Charles came to talk to him. He told him about his plan to form a company to buy land in the industrial area of Tokyo. This area was destroyed by the fire storm and was worthless at this time. He wanted him to head up a company with the idea of purchasing as much of this land as possible. He and Hideaki would be majority owners. The idea frightened him, but his being able to be with his lost family was too exciting. He thought how he could get comfortable with this kind of experience. He decided that all he needed to do was to pretend it was a game. Learn the rules, and play the game well. This got him through the first part of this adventure.

As time passed, he realized that he was in the real world and was successful. Slowly, he was changing. The real change came in 1956. He took his whole family to their meeting at the Mayo Clinic. The warmth of Charles and Lillian, and the joy of Ayame launched him from his cocoon, and he went rapidly into the butterfly. The change in his treatment of his daughters and their husbands was just short of miraculous. His family became openly happy. Chiase and Chie became over night the happy playful girls of the language school days. They reunited with Akemi and Asami. They were the A.C. Girls again. He gave more responsibilities to his son-in-laws. He found that they had much to offer the company. Charles and Hideaki rejoiced over this change.

CHAPTER 17

Hideaki was making progress in his ability to develop a successful company. The skill that he demonstrated at the school impressed the Yokohama Police Department. Charles noted this and told Hideaki that he felt that he should start a security company. He said, "Lillian and I have put aside some money, and we will help you financially." Hideaki said, "I can only accept this if you will be a part owner of the company." Charles said, "This is not necessary as I want you to own the company entirely." Hideaki said, "I will only do it if you will accept 50% of the company." Charles finally accepted 20% of the company.

At the same time this was happening, Charles wrote Dan, his father-in-law, a long letter stating that there were large areas of Tokyo destroyed, and the land could be bought cheaply. He said, "Akihiko, Hideaki, and I are forming a real estate company. Akihiro's surname is Okada, so the company's name will be Okada, Fugimaki, and Bettendorf, Inc. I feel that owning land in Tokyo will be, in a short time, very valuable. I feel it would be wise for you to invest with us."

Dan had seen that the main industrial area of Tokyo had been destroyed. It was obvious that this land would be valuable as Japan recovered. Several letters went back and forth. Bill and Joe got involved. Charles said, "Akihiko and Hideaki will be the primary owners as they are Japanese citizens and will be living in the Tokyo-Yokohama area." Continuing, he said, "I will leave Japan in the near future, and it will be many years before I can return. This means that you and Lucy will be passive partners and will be completely dependent upon Akihiko's and Hideaki's ability and honesty." Dan had met both of these men, but he had no feelings about their ability. His decision would have to be based on Charles' judgment.

Charles told Lillian that he had concerns about asking Dan to invest. He knew that this was a very good investment for them, and he felt it would help her father in his retirement. Lillian knew these two men very well. She had a loving relationship with Ayame and Aiko. Her experience with Hideaki and his search for a religion had impressed her of his character. She said, "Akihiko has always been more reserved with me, but I trust him. He is a very intelligent man, and I feel he will be well qualified to run a real estate firm." She continued by saying, "Both men will not be dependent on the firm for income. They both have their own work. Besides, they are married to very intelligent women, who can help them in managing the real estate. Charles, you have given a clear picture of the risks. It is now my parent's responsibility as to whether they invest or not. As for me, I think we should invest as much as we can."

Dan wrote saying he wanted to participate. The ending structure of the company was with Akihiko owning 35%, Hideaki 25%, Charles and Lillian 25% and Dan 15%. These percentages were based on the amount of time and money that each would spend on the project. All were satisfied with the final structure. Akihiko and Hideaki were deeply touched and honored by Charles and Lillian's trust in them.

It was now July, 1946. MacArthur was finally pleased with the new Japanese Constitution. The clause that Japan would align itself with the United States policies and would have no military reassured him. Japan would be placed under the United States for its military commitments. This satisfied America's fear of a resurgent militarism in Japan. The appointment of Yoshida assured all that under his leadership, Japan would concentrate on rebuilding its industrial based.

As 1946 was winding down, several forces were developing that would change Charles and Lillian's lives. MacArthur decided that the language school was no longer necessary. It was to be closed by the end of 1946. This would work out well for most of the teachers there as they had begun returning to their previous teaching position. The food problem was improving, and there was some construction of housing taking place. Lillian was very busy in helping distribute food and other necessities to the Japanese people. Her activities came to the attention of the Prime Minister's office. Yoshida asked to meet with her. He was pleased when he learned that she was the wife of Captain Bettendorf. He told her how pleased he was with her work and how much it had benefited so many Japanese people. Charles wrote a long letter to her family telling, what had happened.

CHAPTER 18

The other events involved Hideaki. When the Japanese soldiers returned, there was no work and no way to survive using their skills. Many had been successful combat officers. It was inevitable that they would form criminal gangs. The Soviet Union was trying to destabilize the Japanese government so as to develop a communist political party. They needed these gangs to mobilize people for riots and other protests in support of communism. It was controlling the mob like activities and dealing with the criminal gangs that were driving Hideaki's security business. He had been hiring the men from his old combat unit to assist him in managing his growing business. He spent many hours re-educating his men. He made sure that they no longer believed in the deity of the Emperor. He told them they could be tough men and still be caring persons. He used Captain Bettendorf as an example of a tough soldier, who when the war was over, was a kind and generous person. He said, "We will be tough with criminals, but we will not be cruel." This was a hard concept for his ex-soldiers to understand. It was going to take a long time for them to really absorb it.

Yoshida heard about this security company and requested that Hideaki come to his office. Hideaki when he received this request went immediately to Charles and said, "I do not like governments. You own part of this company. I need you to go with me when I go to meet Yoshida." Charles agreed to go with him. Yoshida greeted them warmly and thanked them for coming. Hideaki was surprised by his warmth, and his concern of having an imperial encounter abated. After the usual pleasantries, Yoshida wanted to know more about Hideaki's security company. He had learned of his amazing results. The skills of his company in protecting his clients from mobs and the Japanese mafia were significant. Yoshida said, "Our government is going to form a national police force patterned after the FBI of the United States. I want you to help organize this force." Hideaki said he didn't want to give up his company. He would be willing to advise Yoshida as to its formation, and he could recruit good men to fill their requirements. As far as patterning after the FBI, he would have to go to the FBI Headquarters in the United States in order to study their techniques and organization. He continued saying, "I do not speak English well. The only way I will go is for Captain Bettendorf to go as my interpreter and advisor."

Yoshida listened carefully and thanked them for coming. He said he would think about Hideaki's position and get back with both of them. Several days passed. Charles and Hideaki said nothing to their wives. It was late on a Friday afternoon when they were both requested to come to Yoshida's office. A limousine was sent for them. Yoshida had been conferring with MacArthur about the proposals of Hideaki. MacArthur liked the idea of a Japanese security organization being influenced by his own FBI. The idea that Captain Bettendorf would be his interpreter reassured him about Hideaki. The discovery that Hideaki and his family had become Christians clinched the deal. MacArthur felt that Bettendorf needed to be above company grade level to be effective. He immediately raised him to a Field Grade Major. He issued orders that Bettendorf was to be transferred to Washington, D.C., with the above mission being his duty.

When they arrived at Yoshida's office, they were confronted with all of the above information. Hideaki and Charles said, "It will take a few weeks for us to get ready to go." Hideaki had to get his second in command in a position so that he could manage his company in his absence. Aiko and her girls would go, and this created more problems. Charles and Lillian were thrilled. They were going home. Lillian would be closer to her family. When their letter arrived to Dan and Lucy saying that they would be coming to Washington, D.C., they were very excited. This time Dan was not amazed. Charles was two months shy of his 21st birthday, and he was a Major.

It was mid-October, 1946, when all of this took place. Charles' language school was closed. He and Lillian had little to do in preparation for leaving Japan. Much of their efforts were involved with teaching the Hideaki family a working English. They were finding that Japanese people had difficulty pronouncing certain English alphabetical letters. For example, there is no "L" sound in the Japanese language. Hideaki would pronounce "lemon" as "remon". Take the word "salad". He pronounced it "sarada". He would add a vowel to the end of words. Another problem was English words with two consonants together, i.e. "strawberry". He would pronounce it "sutoroberi". The two girls were interested in words like "hamburger". They pronounced it "hambaagaa". These difficulties troubled Charles and Lillian. They tried many different ways to overcome this. They had to settle with the fact that they were limited English teachers. They concentrated on words they could pronounce, and in three weeks, they could speak crude English. This difficulty made it even more important that Hideaki had an interpreter with whom he had complete trust. Finally, in mid-November, they were ready to leave.

This time Charles would be going on a passenger ship. It was two years ago when he was just nineteen years old, that he had sailed from San Francisco Bay. It took fifty days to get to Leyte and more than a week to get to Japan. Now, they were on a luxury liner, and he had a state room with a beautiful wife. As he reviewed all of the past two years, he could hardly grasp, what had happened to him. Lillian noticed that he was in deep thought and asked, "What are you thinking?" He said, "First, I was thinking of finding you and somehow convincing you to love me." Lillian replied, "You may think it was all your effort, but I will have you know I saw a good thing, and I was not going to let you get away." Laughingly, they hugged each other.

The ocean trip was to last ten days. They sighted land just outside San Juan Straits. It was late in the day, and the days were short. During the night, the ship docked near Seattle. When they awoke that morning, they were home in America.

Hideaki and Aiko had different feelings when they left Japan. Their feelings were like Charles' when he left San Francisco. They were concerned about the strangeness they were about to experience, and at times, they felt some fear. The girls had no such feelings. They were excited about the ship. The idea of going to the United States was just great. As the day ended and as they were entering the San Juan Straits, Hideaki and Aiko stood alone on the stern deck of the ship. They could see Washington State on the right, and on the left, Canada. They thought what a strange feeling they were having. Both had traveled abroad. He went to the South Pacific and, finally, to the Philippines. Aiko went only to the Philippines. They were entering a country he, Hideaki, had fought against and who had defeated him. He muttered to himself about the strange turn of events. Aiko heard his mutterings and asked, "What are you thinking?" He didn't reply with what he had been thinking but replied with the thought that came to his mind when she interrupted his thoughts. He said, "I was thinking of being in a strange place with the woman I love." Aiko could read his thoughts most of the time. She said, "I know that is not what you were muttering about, but I adore what you said." They both hugged and kissed. This sharing washed away all of their fears, and now for the first time, they felt that they could conquer the world.

Getting off the boat was trying for both families. They had to locate their luggage and go through customs. Charles was in his uniform and there was no problem. Lillian, being his wife, caused no problems. Neither one had a passport as they had left the United States during war times. For Hideaki and his family, it was another problem. They had Japanese passports. This was the first time that the custom official had admitted a Japanese national. Charles had realized that this might cause a problem, so he got MacArthur's headquarters to send a memo to the custom officials of Seattle about the coming of Hideaki Fujimaki and his family. When he saw the hold up of Hideaki, he immediately went to the chief customs officer and reminded him of that memo. The chief officer immediately admitted Hideaki with apologies. Hideaki was greatly relieved knowing that Charles was with him.

The Japanese government had worked out the transportation in the United States. They left Seattle and went east through the Cascades to Spokane. From Spokane, they went across Montana and North Dakota ending up in Minneapolis, Minnesota. It was early December, and the ground was covered with snow. They were all glad that they had warm winter clothes. From Minneapolis, they went to Chicago. Hideaki's family was amazed at the size of Charles' country. The large cities were impressive. All of the industry that Hideaki saw impressed him. He said, "No wonder the United States defeated Japan." From Chicago, they went to Pittsburg and onto Washington, D.C. This journey was done entirely by railroads. Washington, D.C. was impressive to all. Hideaki went immediately to the Japanese embassy and was to stay there during his stay in Washington.

Charles was to report to the Pentagon for any new instructions. There were none, and he was told where he and Lillian would be staying. It was close to the Japanese embassy, so the two families could connect easily. It had been a four-day trip and both families were tired. It was late Thursday afternoon when they finally settled in.

Lillian could hardly wait to call her family. There was much joy expressed by both. Her older brothers were home from college and wanted to talk to Charles. They had a great conversation, and ended in them saying they could hardly wait to meet each other face to face.

Charles had avoided talking to Lillian about his family. Since they were back in the states, he felt it was time to talk about his family and the difficulty he had relating to them. He started by saying his mother and father should never have married. His mother was orphaned when she was six years old. She was raised by a half sister, who had not liked her mother. This half sister was attached to her father and resented his marriage to a younger woman, who was only seven years older than she was. His mother was unhappy all of her life.

His father had lost his father when he was fourteen years old. He quit school in the sixth grade. He became the main supporter of his parent family. He had continued this up to the present. Charles said, "I have one sister, and we both got away from our parents as soon as possible." Charles continued saying, "I left home for college at the age of sixteen and haven't gone back except to be drafted. There was no love ever expressed between my parents. My mother was too passive for there to be any arguments. Mother loved us, but she could only feed and clothe us. She could not emotionally support us. My father was always critical of me and was only proud of me when I received my two medals. My mother had written me a letter about my father bragging to his friends about his son."

He further stated that his father would leave the house in early morning and return late at night. This was not related to his work. He ended by saying his father had a lady friend and drank whiskey heavily. Charles said to Lillian with great feeling, "Every time I think of my family, I feel angry and sad. It is so painful for me to talk about my family. I feel badly for a long time afterwards." Lillian said, "Charles, I love you, and I am going to help you get over this painful story. I know my love will get you past this, and we never need to talk about this again." Charles did call his parents and told them he was back in the states in Washington, D.C. They asked if he was coming home and he said a simple "No". This ended the conversation.

Saturday and Sunday were exploring times for the two families. The girls wanted to go to the movies and to eat hamburgers, hot dogs, and pop corn. They had finally learned to pronounce hamburgers almost well enough to be recognized by the waitresses. Hideaki and Aiko were not so adventurous in trying out their English. It was a fun time, and on Sunday, Lillian led the two families to an Episcopal Church, and they all took communion. Monday would be a different day for all of them. The girls would go to the embassy school, and Lillian and Aiko would do the necessary shopping. They had brought very limited clothing with them. Charles and Hideaki were off to the FBI building.

The next three months were filled with conferences with heads of the many divisions of the FBI. Charles was with Hideaki during all of their interviews. As the days went by, Hideaki was more and more able to understand English. He could understand English better than he could speak it. He told Charles that he could not stop thinking in Japanese. When he had to speak, he first said it in Japanese, and then he had to translate to English. This slowed his thinking, and sometimes led to confusion.

After three months, Hideaki felt that he had enough information. Many of the activities of the FBI were not applicable to Japan in its present condition. He concentrated mostly on criminal behavior and subversive activities. He studied mob management. He was surprised that he felt he knew more than they did in mob management. He notified his embassy that he was ready to return to Japan. He requested that he be able to choose the way he would return to Japan. He informed Yoshida that he wanted to return by way of England and Germany. He wanted to see how Scotland Yard worked, and he wanted to see how Germany was reconstructing their federal police. From Germany, he wanted to go by ship through the Suez Canal to Singapore and then on to Japan. He said it would take about 45 days. This kind of journey would help him think on an international scale. Continuing he said he felt that Japan could be again an important nation. It would need men in government that had wide experiences. Yoshida knew that Hideaki was planning to work with the government.

Lillian, Aiko, and the girls spent those three months shopping and exploring. Lillian continued to try to teach them English. She was very successful with the girls. They loved being in America. Aiko had the same trouble as Hideaki. She could not stop thinking in Japanese first. When it became a fact that they would be leaving Washington on the 31st of March, 1947, they spent the last week buying items that they would need and which would be scarce in Japan. They avoided talking about leaving Charles and Lillian as even a slight thinking about it brought emotional pain.

Charles and Hideaki handled it differently. They knew that they would be involved with each other through their businesses and their need for each other's friendship. They felt that they were brothers in arms even though they had fought each other. When they parted, they kissed each other's cheeks. They gave each other a strong hug.

With Lillian and Aiko, it was different. They were very emotional. They were sisters now, and they could read each other's thoughts as if they had been sisters all of their lives. Their husbands had to pull them apart as the last call to board the train had been called. So, slowly the train pulled away with all of them clinging to the last glimpse of each other. As Charles and Lillian walked away, Lillian was crying, and Charles said, "It seems to me that the people staying behind have the most pain as they go back to the usual while the departers are starting a new adventure."

Over the next 45 days, Charles and Lillian received cards from London, Bonn, Germany; Cairo, Bombay, and Singapore. When Hideaki and Aiko got to Tokyo, each wrote long letters about their trip and what was happening in Japan. Hideaki wrote about their businesses saying they were doing very well, and Akihiko was still buying real estate. Hideaki said that his security business was doing so well that he was going to send Charles some of the profits. Charles replied, "Don't send money. Invest our surplus back into the company."

When Hideaki left, Charles' detached service ended. He had no connections with the Pentagon. He had read that Congress was insisting that the Army reduce its forces. With this in mind, Charles applied for early retirement. The Army accepted his request with the condition that he would serve the remaining part of his enlistment in the active reserve. That meant on June 15, 1950, he would be relieved of his Army obligations.

CHAPTER 19

For the first time, Charles and Lillian were having ordinary life experiences. Charles was still planning to become a medical doctor. He had gotten some credits for pre-med at Tokyo University. In January, 1947, he had enrolled in Georgetown University and had completed two trimesters. After one more trimester, then he would be eligible to apply for medical school. His last day of active duty was June 1, 1947. He took some leave time so that he was able to start attending summer school at Vanderbilt University on June 1st.

They had left Washington as soon as he finished his classes at Georgetown. He had kept in touch with Dr. Mayfield and his grades, according to Dr. Mayfield, qualified him to be considered for Vanderbilt Medical School. There was one problem. Charles could not apply until he knew he would be released from the Army. When he was able to apply, the class was already filled.

Dr. Mayfield was aware of this. He admired what Charles had done for his country. He had strong feelings that Charles should be admitted to medical school that fall. He personally took Charles' scholastic record to the admissions committee and to the head of the medical school. He knew that the current head was an ex-general, who had fought in the war. Dr. Mayfield had difficulty with the admissions committee. When he presented his war record to the General, there was no question about him being admitted. Charles received his acceptance to the 1947 class.

Now, they had to start thinking how they were going to support themselves for the next four years. They would have his GI Bill to help with tuition and part of their living expenses. Lillian also wanted to finish her college. This would create a greater problem. Charles felt that after the freshman year, he could find some extra work. Lillian was thinking the same for her.

One day Charles was visiting with Dr. Mayfield. He was talking about his language school in Tokyo. Dr. Mayfield hadn't known about this. He asked Charles how fluent was he in the Japanese language. He replied that he could speak, read, and write it. Furthermore, the Foreign Minister of Japan had used his skills repeatedly. He inquired if Charles could teach Japanese to students. Charles said, "My students were Army officers from MacArthur's headquarters." Mayfield was becoming excited as Vanderbilt had no one to teach Japanese. As he listened, he wondered how he could test Charles in such a way that the school would consider him as a qualified teacher. Charles had no academic credentials to present. He asked, "Charles, what can we do that would convince the faculty that you are qualified to teach Japanese?" Charles thought of the Japanese ambassador in Washington. When he called him, he suggested that they use the Japanese Consul located in Nashville, Tennessee.

A committee of faculty members, Dr. Mayfield, and Charles went to the Consul's office to see Charles tested. When they arrived, all sat down but Charles. Charles walked over to the Consul and bowed saying in clear and correct Japanese, "Honorable Consul, it gives me great honor to be in your presence." the Consul returned his greeting and asked Charles to sit down. They had a long chat about Tokyo. The news from Tokyo was so interesting to the Consul that he forgot that he was supposed to be testing. Charles said, "Honorable Consul, I must interrupt our conversation as they have no idea of what we are doing. It is my hope that you can test me in such a way that it will convince them that I am qualified to teach the Japanese language at this school." He replied, "You have already demonstrated your speaking skills." The Consul turned to the faculty members and said, "I talked to your candidate in very complicated Japanese. He performed as well as I could. I will now test reading and writing skills." Charles performed them as well as he had speaking. Everyone was impressed, and Dr. Mayfield was bursting with pride. To him, Charles was his protégé. The faculty voted to appoint him a fellow in Japanese language and gave him a job teaching Japanese. At this point, Charles told them that Lillian's skills equaled his, and he wondered if she could have an appointment, also. They agreed, and now they had paying jobs. Lillian would have her tuition waivered.

September came and they were back in college as students and teachers. Charles' first year of medical school involved the taking of gross anatomy and microscopic anatomy. These two subjects required long hours of laboratory work. Charles worked out his teaching with his lab schedule. It would mean at times, he would have to work late at night in the anatomy laboratory. His anatomy instructor warned him that he would have no help from the lab instructor when he made up his lab time. Understanding this, Charles had to study much harder than his classmates. The only time Lillian and Charles were together was in the early morning and late at night. This was a hard adjustment for them as they were used to much more togetherness. The four months passed, and final exams were at hand. For one week, all Lillian and Charles did was preparing for and taking exams. When grades came out, Charles had set the curve in all of his courses. Lillian did well in her courses. There had been some doubt that Charles could be a teacher and a medical student at the same time. His grades settled that issue.

At the end of the anatomy class, Vanderbilt Medical School had a tradition called the cadaver ball. All students that had passed anatomy had a celebration dance at a local honky-tonk. This year it was held at a dance hall called "The Plantation Club". It was about eight miles from the campus. It was a cold rainy night, and the road leading to the dance hall was slick and almost impassable. Charles and Lillian made it and had a memorable time. It seemed to them that this was the first time that they were partying with people their own age.

CHAPTER 20

All year Lillian had longed to visit her family. The Christmas holidays were the time when they were going to her home. It was an exciting trip to Athens, Georgia. Lillian had not been with her family for over two years. Her parents had visited them in January, 1946. The only contact with the rest of the family was through pictures and mail. Her two younger brothers and sister were finishing high school and grade school. Her two older brothers were out of under graduate school and had entered law school and graduate school for business.

It was late in the afternoon when they arrived. The Kenworth family was happy, and Lillian introduced Charles as the newest member of their family. The older brothers couldn't wait to get to talk with Charles. They were amazed at what a tall, well formed, handsome man he was. It was no surprise to them that he was also very intelligent. They had planned hunting trips for Charles, and they had no idea how he would perform.

Charles, in youth, was an accomplished hunter. His skill with a 22 caliber rifle in hunting squirrels was impressive. With a 22 caliber rifle, he could hit a running squirrel in its head at 150 feet with one shot. He was a great stalker of deer. So, early the next morning, they went deer hunting. Charles inquired how many deer were they allowed to kill. They smiled at the request as they didn't expect Charles even to see a deer. They told Charles to stay at his stand and wait for a deer to come. Charles asked,

"What direction are your stands?" He wanted to know their firing zones. He didn't want to shoot them or they shoot him. With this exchange, they parted.

It was about ten o'clock when they heard a gunshot far off in the distance. They thought at least one hunter was getting a shot at a deer. When noon came, they decided to call the morning hunt off and go to Charles' stand. When they got to his stand, they saw a gutted deer hanging from a tree limb. It was a 12 point buck. They were dumbfounded. They thought that they were going to have to look out for Charles and now this. Charles explained that he had looked around the stand and could find no signs of deer passing his stand. He knew where his brothers' stands were and decided to explore the woods south of their stands. He thought that he must have gone about two miles when he found deer tracks. He placed himself in a tall tree and waited. He said, "About 10 o'clock, this 12 point buck appeared. There were three does with him." Continuing he said, "I had to wait about 30 minutes to get a clear shot." His brother-in-laws felt foolish as it was obvious Charles was an experienced hunter. They insisted on carrying the buck out of the woods to their pickup. They proudly placed the deer so all could see what a successful hunt they had. When they stopped at the tagging station, the deer was greatly admired. They proudly stated that their brother-in-law had tracked down this deer and had killed it with one shot.

This Christmas was their first Christmas with Lillian's family. Charles' memories of his family's Christmases were generally unhappy experiences. He thought what a difference Lillian had made in his life. This Christmas was joyful, and for the first time, he felt cheerful about Christmas. The holidays ended too soon, and they were heading back to Nashville, Tennessee.

The second semester was much easier for Charles. Lillian would start her first year in nursing school in the fall. When final exams came, Charles again set the curve. Charles' classmates were upset with his high grades. His setting the curve so high meant their grades were lower. When they confronted Charles about this, he said, "I am not trying to make high grades, I just want to learn as much as I can." They had to settle with this explanation. The overall effect was that all had to study harder. Summer came, and they taught summer school for advanced Japanese language students.

Lillian did well in her first year. She did not set the curve. That summer they went to Athens, Georgia. By this time, Lillian had shown off Charles to everyone in Athens, and he felt that Athens was his home.

In the summer of 1948, Charles and Lillian received a letter from Hideaki and Aiko. It was written in English. They wrote about many things, but the real reason was regarding Akemi. She was 19 and wanted to study in the United States. Her interests were in political science and business. She wanted to come to Vanderbilt University. She was a student at Tokyo University, and they included her credits from that school. Both parents said that they would only consent to this if she could stay with them. They ended the letter by reporting that they could speak English now, and they no longer pronounced lemon as remon or put vowels at the end of words. Needless to say, Charles and Lillian were pleased and excited.

They immediately replied with a resounding "yes", and started the process of getting Akemi admitted to Vanderbilt. Charles felt the best strategy was to say that a friend of theirs wanted to come to Vanderbilt University. She would be a great help in their Japanese language courses. Continuing, they told admissions that she spoke perfect English. Her grades were superior and there was no problem getting her admitted for the fall term of 1948.

Akemi's coming meant that they were going to have to get a larger place. When she arrived, they were surprised by the change. She was a beautiful young lady. She had arrived just a week before classes began. She was very adaptable and a joy to be with. Akemi was quick to tell them that she only intended to stay with them one semester. She said her parents would not have let her come if she had not agreed to spend the first semester with them. She wanted to have a typical student experience, and this included living in a dormitory or her own apartment. There was no money problem for her family.

When her first semester was up, she moved into a dormitory. She had a roommate, Alice Cate, who came from Texas. They hit it off quite well from the beginning. Akemi was a very beautiful young lady and was sought after by all of the sororities. She chose Kappa Alpha Theta. She didn't need a sorority to get dates. She was very popular. Akemi was more interested in her political science studies than in becoming involved with any of the young men available. It was only in her second year that she met a young man in the student lounge. He happened to be standing at a book stand, that had a book she was trying to find. The book was about the political situation in Japan during the MacArthur period. As it turned out, he was reading that book. When they discovered this coincidence, they started talking with each other. Both were interested as to why each sought the same book.

Akemi started first by saying she was studying political science and was wondering what the political situation was for the Japanese during the MacArthur administration. Up to this point, Daniel Petrie had not noticed that she was Japanese. To him, she was a beautiful young woman, and he wanted to get her name. Hopefully, he could get a date. Akemi went on to say that she was here at Vanderbilt because her uncle was a student at Vanderbilt Medical School. At that time, she went no further. To her, he was a handsome young man, but there was nothing particularly interesting about him.

Daniel started relating his reason for looking up this book. He said that his father was in the Pacific in World War II. He had heard many times about his experiences in Japan. He told me about a friend, who worked in the headquarters of MacArthur. His stories about the political turmoil during this period interested him. He said he had a free period, and he had decided to go to the bookstore and look up some books on this period. Continuing, he said, "I have a distant relationship with my father. My father was overseas during the formative years of my life. We never got close. I admire my father, and that is why I am looking up the periods when my father was away."

Akemi had lost her father in the war. He had never loved her, and this story sounded familiar. Her stepfather dearly loved her, and he had given her the courage to be strong and independent. After a few minutes, Daniel asked, "Akemi, would you like to have a coke with me?" His story of estrangement with his father attracted her. She agreed. They talked for several hours, and the more they talked the more interested they became in each other. It was late afternoon when they became aware it was time for dinner.

Daniel was a junior, and he did not live in the dormitories. He ate at the local restaurants. He told her that his favorite place was Hank's on Elliston Place. She had heard of this hang out for Vandy students. She had never been there. She had decided that she wanted to know more about this young man and said she would go with him. This was the beginning of many dates over the next few months.

There were follow up letters from Hideaki. He reported that his business was improving very much, and soon he would have enough surplus cash that he could start sending dividends to Charles. The rest of 1948 continued with Charles, Lillian and Akemi doing well in their studies. Akemi was a big help in teaching Japanese.

By the spring semester, Akemi was going steady with a young man from Texas. Charles knew the Japanese customs for couples, who are courting, and he was concerned about their growing interest in each other. This young man's name was Daniel Petrie. This last name was startling to Charles. Could he be connected to Captain Petrie? It didn't take long for Charles to find out the answer. When Akemi brought Daniel over to meet them, Charles got around to asking where in Texas he lived. Daniel said, "I come from Nacogdoches." Charles knew this was where Captain Petrie had lived. In the next few minutes, he knew that Daniel was the son of his dear friend and comrade. When Charles told him that he was a close friend of his father, Daniel became very excited. He said, "My father talks about you all of the time." He further stated that his father had been trying for a long time to find you.

With that, Charles immediately called Sam. They had a long talk and when Charles related how he had found him, he asked, "Did you know that your young son is interested in my ward, Akemi?" Charles said, "Do you remember that hostile Colonel that you were having trouble disarming?" Sam replied, "You mean that one that I called on you for help because he refused to talk in English or have an interpreter?" Charles replied, "Yes, that is the one. It is his daughter that brought your son to meet us. Akemi is very dear to Lillian and me. We are very close to her parents. It is our connection with them that brought Akemi to Vanderbilt." Sam said, "I sent Daniel to Vanderbilt for one reason. I remembered your talking about Vanderbilt and your intention to go there for medical school. When Daniel said he wanted to be a doctor, I told him if I was paying for his school, he would go to Vanderbilt."

Daniel was going to graduate in pre-med in two years, and Sam was hoping to see Charles and Lillian both before that. Charles said it would be sooner. Maybe this summer he and Lillian could drive down to Nacogdoches.

The rest of Daniel's visit was filled with Charles, Lillian, and Daniel talking continuously. Finally, Akemi interrupted and said, "This meeting was not supposed to be a reunion, but it was supposed to be my introducing Daniel to my surrogate parents according to Japanese culture." Continuing, she said, "I had told Daniel that you would be very formal, and to an American, you might be considered slightly hostile. Now, look at what has happened. Daniel will have no understanding of how Japanese couples meet." She broke out laughing and said, "I am so pleased that our first meeting has been so American." She went further by saying that young Japanese people were breaking away from traditions connected with the Emperor being a deity. Besides, her family was Christian, and Shinto customs were no longer a part of their lives.

That summer three things happened. First, when Hideaki and Aiko realized that their oldest daughter was engaged to an American, they wrote Charles and said, "We will be in Nashville in early June. We are going to take Akemi to Nacogdoches about the same time." Second, it was decided that all three families would be together in Nacogdoches. The third event was a private event. Lillian told Charles that she was 25 years old, and she did not want to delay having a family. She wanted to start immediately trying to get pregnant. Charles was pleased and didn't discuss his concern of starting a family when they had such limited resources.

The spring came and went, and June came. Aiko and Hideaki arrived, and they stayed in Nashville for a few days enjoying just being together again. Aiko and Hideaki were concerned about the possibility of their daughter's marriage to an American as it would be a mixture of two cultures. They lamented that if Daniel was more like Charles and had Charles' know how of their culture, there would be less cultural problems. There was no way that they could relieve themselves of these concerns. Charles suggested waiting until they met Daniel and his family. They felt that Aiko and Hideaki should be openly expressive of their concerns to the couple and to Daniel's family.

During all of these conversations, Charles reminded Hideaki about his connection with Captain Petrie. He had no fond memories of this encounter. About the 15th of June, they left for Nacogdoches, Texas.

Daniel had gone before them. He and Akemi had their talk with her parents and their mutual concerns were expressed. Akemi's parents were surprised at how much Akemi and Daniel had talked about how complicated their love for each other would be for their parents.

During the trip to Texas, Charles and Hideaki talked about their company and their investments with Akihiko. He reported that his business was progressing very well. His connection with the Japanese Federal Police was very helpful, both from consulting fees and added business that he got from those connections. He said, "By next year, I will be putting you on salary." Charles asked, "Is this wise?" Hideaki replied, "If business continues as well as it has, I will have more than enough money to expand our business. I feel that it is time for you to get some benefit from your investment." Charles thanked him and said, "Lillian wants to start our family. She doesn't want to be a middle aged mother." They both laughed for Lillian was only 26 and Aiko was in her early forties and pregnant.

Hideaki looked at Charles and said, "Charles, there is no age prejudice about you. You seem to be the age of the person that you are talking to. You are an unusual fellow. I thank God for helping me find you. Many nights Aiko and I talk about you and Lillian. Certainly, without Lillian, we would never have met."

It took about fourteen hours to get to Nacogdoches. Daniel was waiting on the porch. His parents said, "He has been standing on the porch for the last two hours." Akemi's and Daniel's greetings were heartwarming. Their glow was infectious.

Hideaki had been concerned about meeting Sam Petrie. Charles had advised him to address him with his first name. The hope was that they could find common grounds that did not include their war experiences. Both had been infantry commanders. Hideaki had been a regimental commander, and Sam was company grade. Both had had hard fighting and had lost close friends. Sam had the same concerns.

Daniel had told him that Akemi was going to be his wife, and he wanted both families to get along. Daniel's mother, Mary, also urged Sam to have at least an open mind. Daniel's family had not seen pictures of Akemi or her parents and had wondered if they were colored yellow and had slant eyes. Daniel sensed their concerns and told them Akemi and her parents were no darker than they were if they had a summer tan. As far as her eyes, he felt that Akemi's eyes were very beautiful. All of these concerns vanished in the first few minutes of getting acquainted.

Since Charles and Lillian had never met Mary, they had much to share with her. At the beginning Charles, Sam, and Hideaki got together as did Lillian, Aiko, and Mary. The men avoided war talk and found that their business interests and recreational activities were enough to give them time to see how close they could be with each other. This only applied to Sam and Hideaki.

The women had no problem relating with each other. Their activities were around their families. When they started talking about children, Lillian had to tell them that they were going to start having children and that she wanted to have at least four. She wanted two boys and two girls. Mary had three children and Aiko had three. Aiko and Hideaki were expecting a baby in six months. They had left Asami in Tokyo with her relatives. If it was a boy, he would be named Charles Yosuka. She said,

"Hideaki insists on this." It was so easy for them to feel close to each other. It would take longer for Sam and Hideaki.

Akemi was a hit with both of Daniel's parents. They thought that she was a very beautiful young lady, and she would be a very good addition to their family. At this time Aiko and Hideaki had not gotten that far in accepting Daniel as a son-in-law. All in all, it was a good beginning for both families. They all decided they would just sit back and let things happen, and if prejudices came up, "they would brand that cow when it happened". That was Sam's expression. As a hobby, he had started a ranch and had put about one hundred mother cows on it. He said, "I am trying to learn cowboy language." The men had gone to the ranch and had ridden around the ranch. In the past, Hideaki had been in the Emperor's Guard and had to be a competent rider. Charles had ridden a horse from the age twelve to sixteen, so there were no tenderfoots in the crowd. A sign of how well things had gone was the nostalgia felt as they left.

Before they left, Charles and Sam called David Jones. He had gotten home and was doing well. He wanted them to come to Lamesa, but the distance was too great, and time was short. Charles wanted him and his family to come to Nashville and spend some time with them. They couldn't decide on a date.

Akemi was going to stay behind and planned to return to Nashville with Daniel at the start of the fall term. As the two couples were driving back, they were pleased about how well things had gone. There were still reservations on Aiko and Hideaki's part, but they were not going to interfere.

When they reached Nashville, Lillian had missed her second period, and she was sure that she was pregnant. This was going to be her secret for a little longer as she wanted to be alone with Charles when she made her announcement. Shortly after they got back to Nashville, Hideaki and Aiko left for home. They had decided that they would come to the United States yearly if Akemi's engagement progressed. The parting this time was more pleasant because they would be seeing each other regularly.

A short time later, Charles received a letter from Akihiko. He informed him that he had made a large profit on a sale of a lot in the industrial district, and he would be sending regular dividends to Charles and Lillian's family. So, in the fall of 1949, Charles started his junior year in med school. The next year would be different because Lillian was pregnant and finishing her second year in nursing. Things went well, and Lillian's mother came to help Lillian after the baby was born on May 11, 1950. With Lucy's help, the baby boy rapidly adjusted to his family. Two months before, Aiko wrote they had a baby boy, and his name was Charles. When the baby was sleeping all night, Lucy went home. Akemi was going to help baby sit when Lillian and Charles had classes. There were problems, but they worked them out.

As the school year ended, the news from Korea became more of a concern to Lillian and Charles. He was still in the active reserve and would be until June fifteenth. Finally, that time came and passed. They were relieved, but they did not receive a notice of his discharge. The Pentagon foresaw the possibility of war and had extended his obligation without notifying him. Lillian and he were sure that he was now out of the reserve and didn't react on June 25, 1950.

War broke out between North and South Korea. It was early the next morning when he received a telegram stating that he was to report immediately to Fort Benning, Georgia. He was to assume command of a forming infantry battalion. It was a shock to both of them as he had just finished his third year in medical school. Charles immediately called the personnel department of the Pentagon. He eventually got in touch with the department that issued his orders to report to Fort Benning. He first stated that he had finished his five years post war obligation on the 15th of June, 1950. They said, "On the 5th of June we extended your obligation under the provision of your enlistment, which says in the case of a national emergency, your obligation can be extended." He told them he was entering his fourth year of medical school, and he wanted his classification changed from infantry to medical. After much debate, his orders were changed to read on completion of medical school, he would get his internship at an army hospital. After that, he would be assigned to an infantry regiment as a battalion surgeon.

CHAPTER 23

The senior year would have been enjoyable if it were not for the Korean War. Both were seniors in their respective schools and would graduate at the same time. Having a baby at this time concerned them. They put off their concern for the time being. Their baby, Sam Hideaki, was a healthy robust boy. He thrived with the attention of his parents and Akemi. Akemi and Daniel were with each other most of the time. Daniel would get involved with baby sitting in order to be with Akemi. Daniel knew that the baby was named after his father and wrote him as soon as the baby's name was announced. Thus Charles received a letter from Sam telling him how pleased he was that they had named their first baby after him. Charles was still leading his class scholastically. He would finish first in his class. Lillian maintained her grades and finished in the top five of her class.

Lillian wrote a long letter to Aiko. She told her about their baby boy and his middle name being Hideaki. She reported how Akemi was such a great help to her, baby sitting. She knew that Aiko wanted to know all about Akemi and Daniel. She told her that Akemi was upset that her mother and father still had reservations about her marrying Daniel. Akemi had been trying to get Lillian to help her get her parent's consent. Lillian told Akemi neither she nor Charles could interfere for her in this area. She related in her letter to Aiko what Akemi had said about her frustration over the lack of approval of Daniel. She told her she thought it would be wise for them to come to Nashville in May, 1951. She felt that Akemi and Daniel might do something rash. Aiko's response came shortly. She said, "Hideaki was elated and very proud about the baby's name." Continuing, she said, "We know we cannot be passive with this issue. We will come in May. This time, we will bring the whole family."

All through his senior year, Charles was constantly following the news about the war. He would read the casualties list and would many times read names of men with whom he had served. He knew when the United States troops were withdrawn from South Korea in 1949, South Korea would be unable to defend itself. In the early stages of the war, the South Koreans had no armor and no air force. What really disturbed him were the battles of Osan and Taejon. In these battles, the American 24th Division was severely defeated and lost 3,602 men and 2,962 captured including the division commander, Major General William F. Dean. In August and September, 1950, Charles watched in despair the Battle of Pusan. He was disturbed by the fact that General MacArthur did not ever go to Korea. In September, the Incheon Landing was accomplished, and it seemed for a while the war would be over.

When MacArthur ordered the troops to go north of the 38th parallel, he again became fearful. At first, things went well. By October 25, 1950, there were encounters with the Chinese Army. On November 1, 1950, Chinese General Pei's forces attacked in a three prong maneuver and overwhelmed the ROK (Republic of Korean armed forces) and the advanced units of the Eighth Army. This began the longest retreat that an American Army had ever had in its history.

By Christmas, Charles knew that he would be going to Korea. What disturbed him most was the American soldiers were abandoning their wounded, and many battalion surgeons were establishing perimeters around their aid stations. They were in fact defending their wounded as their own troops had abandoned them. He knew one such battalion surgeon personally. He had defended his station and saved his wounded soldiers' lives. He was awarded a Bronze Star.

Things seemed to stabilize until the Chinese winter offensive began in January, 1951. The Chinese utilized night attacks and stealthily encircled American positions. Using the element of surprise and overwhelming numbers of troops, they over ran positions. By January 4, 1951, the Chinese recaptured Seoul. At this time, their tactics of having loud trumpets and gongs disoriented many troops and the term "bugged out" became identified with the Korean War. This offensive was stopped by American counter offensives. By March, 1951, Seoul had been retaken, and the Chinese fourth phase offensive had been stopped. A stale mate was established. All of this cast a dark cloud over Charles and Lillian's lives.

In May, 1951, Charles and Lillian graduated. He was the top graduate in his class and Lillian was fourth in her class. Charles had applied to only one place for his internship. It was Brooke Army Hospital, San Antonio, Texas.

CHAPTER 24

In late May, Hideaki and Aiko arrived with their boy and Asami. They were committed to bring their problem with Akemi and Daniel to a conclusion. They had long talks with Akemi and Daniel together and separately. They asked Sam and Mary if they would come to Nashville and discuss with them about what their two adult children were insisting on doing. Hideaki was particularly concerned about the prejudice they would experience. He knew that many American veterans still hated the Japanese. He told Sam he was afraid for both Akemi and Daniel. Both parents recognized the fear expressed. Sam said, "I don't know if Daniel's marriage would be accepted in our small Texas town." Hideaki said, "There would be no trouble in Japan as the Japanese are accepting the Americans as being helpful in their recovery." After all of these discussions, both families said they would support them whatever their decision was.

Akemi and Daniel got married and Daniel was to start his first year in Vanderbilt Medical School, and Akemi was to start graduate studies in political science. The issue of support was settled with Hideaki's family supporting Akemi, and Sam's family supporting Daniel. In spite of all the discord, both families were happy with the marriage.

Charles and Lillian packed their things and left for San Antonio, Texas, and Fort Sam Houston. Charles had decided that he was going to apply for a surgical internship. He was aware of the Mash units in Korea, and he intended to join one as soon as his internship was over.

It was a trying time for both of them. Charles was on duty many nights, and he volunteered almost every weekend for emergency room duty. Brooke Army Hospital had an emergency service that attended to many patients with gunshot and stabbing wounds from San Antonio. At first, Charles was a second assistant for these surgeries. As the year passed, he advanced to first assistant, and in times of too many patients, he performed surgery by himself.

In October, Charles received a letter from his father. He wrote that he was having trouble swallowing and wondered what he should do. Charles feared it might mean he had esophageal cancer as his father was a heavy alcoholic, and smoked two to three packages of cigarettes daily. He got emergency leave and went to Little Rock, Arkansas, where his father had been hospitalized. When he arrived, the diagnosis had been made, and his physician had given his father his options. Essentially, he was terminally ill. Doing surgery was considered a heroic gesture with limited potentials. Charles told his dad that dilating the esophagus was his best option.

His father was a different person. He openly expressed that he was proud of him. It was sad for Charles as he had very few pleasant times with his father. Now that he was dying, he was expressing feelings for his son that he had never expressed. His father chose surgery and died two days post op. During those two days, Charles didn't leave his father's side. He knew he probably wouldn't regain consciousness, but he was going to be there if he did. The words his father had said to Lillian echoed in his mind, "I will be buried on Friday." He was. After the burial, Charles brought his mother back to San Antonio.

Lillian was seven months pregnant. When it was evident that Charles would be in the war and likely going overseas, Lillian expressed that she was not going to let circumstances stop her in getting her family started. She had told Charles that she wanted to have her completed family before she was thirty. She had thought that this was going to be easy. The war was going to make it more difficult for her and, ultimately, Charles. He smiled at her determined stand and said, "You don't have to be so determined as I will always be on your side." she burst out in tears and hugged him saying, "Oh, Charles, I love you so much."

Charles' mother, Leah, was a great deal of help for Lillian. Sam was a struggling two year old and into everything. His grandmother was very attentive with him. They played games together and would go to the park and let Lillian sleep. Lillian felt very heavy during her last month of pregnancy. A baby boy was born on December 5, 1951. They named him John William after her older brother.

It was a trying time for all of them. Sam was jealous of the attention his mother gave to the new baby. Charles was overworking himself in his effort to be a skilled trauma surgeon. He had very little time or energy to be of much help. It was during these times that Lillian discovered how much she cared for her mother-in-law. She noticed that she never complained no matter how bad things were. When Lillian was so exhausted and all she could do was cry, Leah was there to help and comfort her. Lillian remembered that Charles had expressed how much he regretted his mother's passiveness. Lillian was seeing this word "passive" in a different light. She saw Leah as a person that persevered when everything seemed hopeless. She felt that she was a loving caring person, and she had a growing love for her.

Lillian was probably the first adult that had felt this way towards Leah, and she responded. She started talking about her childhood and how sad and frightened she was when her mother died. Her emotional support came from her mother. She remembered her father as an old man, who didn't play with her or her brother. The events that followed were devastating. Her half sister considered her a burden. She complained constantly about having to take care of her. She learned to be quiet and not bother her. She said she knew that Charles thought that she was too helpless and passive but that was the only way she could survive. She talked about her marriage. She said that her husband came from a poor family. He saw the apparent wealth of her family and was more interested in that and less so in her. She knew she had to get away from her half sister, so marriage seemed a way. When her husband realized that her half sister had spent all of her inheritance, their relation fell apart. She was back in a persevering structure. Enduring and taking care of her children was all she felt she could do. She wondered many times why didn't she just walk away but being alone reminded her of her mother's death, and she felt paralyzed. Lillian tried to talk to Charles about what she had learned, but he couldn't feel for his mother like she did.

The end of Charles' internship was fast approaching. Charles had contacted the personnel department of the Pentagon and made his request to be assigned to a Mash unit in Korea. He got letters from the chief surgeon of Brooke Army Hospital telling of his qualifications. The letter stated that Charles had more experience in trauma surgery than a third year resident in surgery. With that letter, he was assigned to 8450 Mash Unit located somewhere near the Han River in South Korea.

When his internship finished on the first of June, he was given a two week leave in order to get his affairs in order. This meant getting Lillian and their two boys to Athens, Georgia. He had to find a house for them and set up financial resources that would keep his family with good finances during his absence.

Finally, he took his mother to his sister's home. When Leah was to say goodbye to them, she hugged Lillian and said, "Thank you for being a loving daughter. You have been the only person in my life that I felt really cared for me." Charles was startled by this comment and wondered about himself. They both said that when his tour of duty was over, she must come and live with them. All of Lillian's family was concerned for Charles' safety, and both of the older brothers said, "We will watch after your family."

He left on the fifteenth of June, 1952. He was driven to Atlanta and there took a flight to Los Angeles. He had a lay over until 10:00 p.m. that night. The next flight took a long time, and they landed in Honolulu, Oahu, in the early morning hours. He rested that day and early the next day took a flight to Wake Island. They refueled and flew on to Tokyo. Hideaki and Akihiko met him at the airport. They visited for several Hours. Both were upset that he was going to be in harm's way. Strong feelings had developed between them over the years. Both told him that their companies were doing well and that he had been put on salary with both companies. They would see that Lillian would get his salaries in a timely manner and not to worry because after all, he was their brother. They parted, and he flew to his Mash unit.

That night he was in a new world. He was in a tent with three doctors. The ground was their floor. In fact that whole hospital was a large tent. They were located near the front lines, and he could hear gun fire. He was told that the Eighth Army had learned how to deal with the Chinese tactics of night surroundings. The Eighth Army fought like Charles had fought in his last battle on Luzon. They attacked around the compass and broke up the encirclement creating huge losses to the enemy.

When he arrived, both sides realized they were in a stalemate. They had begun negotiation, but they couldn't resolve the problems of prisoners of war. None of the North Koreans and Chinese prisoners wanted to be returned to their countries. This was unacceptable. When negotiations stopped, the Chinese would attack to see how determined the United Nations were. This would produce casualties and much work for all.

Charles' ability was quickly recognized, and he was considered a surgeon's surgeon.

Lillian missed Charles terribly. When their baby was six months old, she felt that he could travel, so she wrote Aiko. She said, "I am coming to Japan. I am going to get as close to Charles as I can." She asked Aiko to find a place for her. She planned to get there by the end of November. Aiko and Hideaki were delighted to know that she was coming. They replied that they were living on a large estate, and she would have the guest cottage. Hideaki added a note saying he could hardly wait to be with his name child, and he wanted his son and his name child to become friends. Lillian met with all kinds of resistance from her family and Charles. Nothing stopped her, and she arrived on schedule as planned. When Charles realized she was in Japan, he immediately applied for Christmas leave. This was granted. They would be together in three weeks.

This would be the strangest and the happiest Christmas of their lives. They had been separated for six months, and they seemed so different. He had been in harsh abnormal situations with much destruction of bodies and lives. He was insensitive and withdrawn from his emotions. He was afraid to awaken his feelings as shortly he would be returning to hell. He said, "I have to get warm again." Lillian didn't understand what he meant. He tried to be warm and caring, but Lillian knew it wasn't there. They talked, but he couldn't tell her what he was feeling. Lillian went to Hideaki and asked him to talk with Charles. Lillian said, "He relates to me as if he were dead inside." Hideaki knew exactly, what was happening to Charles. He told Lillian a story about his first trip home from combat. He was with his first wife, and he was frozen. He could not get the fear and horror of combat out of his mind. He felt that if he let go and loved again, he could not cope. His protection had been not feeling, and his wife longed for feelings, so she could cope with her loneliness. They were defeating each other. He said, "Lillian, Charles worships you.

Give him time, he will get better. Give him room and he will be like the turtle. He will stick out his head and test the air, and slowly he will be your Charles again." It took almost the entire leave to get there. When he became more loving, he told her he would never let himself get that detached from his emotions. He said, "If I can't do that, I don't need to be a trauma surgeon."

CHAPTER 25

By May, 1953, his two year duty was over, and he was going home. When he heard this, he wondered where he would go for his surgical residency. During his year at his Mash unit, they had at times been visited by prominent surgeons. These men had volunteered to visit the Mash units to see if they could offer advice or help. One of these consultants had impressed Charles. He and Charles seemed to get along well together. He told Charles he wanted him to come to his facility. He would get him a fellowship. This physician was Dr. Ted Holman, and he was head of a general surgery unit at the Mayo Clinic in Rochester, Minnesota. Charles wrote him and said he would be discharged from the Army on June 1, 1953. He would like to come to the Mayo Clinic and study under him. In the next mail, he received an appointment to be a fellow in surgery at the Mayo Clinic.

Lillian was still in Japan when his discharge came. He was on the next flight to Tokyo. This time there was no difficulty for either of them. Aiko and Lillian had become very close with each other. Hideaki told Charles that he and his son were going to have a hard time giving up his name son. They stayed a week and flew to Rochester. The flight was long and hard on all. John William was fussy, but Charles didn't mind. He felt that he had missed a lot of experiences with his two sons and wanted to be a part of their lives. He wanted them to know he was their father. He was determined that he would be different from his father. He was not going to wait until he was dying to show them how much he loved them. Lillian was reunited with the other part of her life and was happy.

All of the newness of being together lessened. They both felt that the loss of one year in their lives together needed to be talked through. Lillian was the first one, who wanted to talk about that year. "When you left," she started saying, "You made me a displaced person. Even though I was with my community and my family, I was a widow woman. I had a three year old son and a baby seven months old. Sam needed his father and I needed help. I needed a husband's help. A baby is very demanding. A break from these demands was like a fresh spring breeze. I had no fresh spring breezes. I lost my friend, lover, and the only person I completely trusted. All of my family realized my distress but were very little comfort. Sam cried for a month about you not being there. It got so bad that I decided that only Aiko would understand what I was experiencing. I wrote her a letter telling her of my feelings. She immediately wrote saying, 'Come to me and Hideaki. We both have lost spouses, and we can share with you how we overcame our distress.' That is why I was so insistent to leave and go to Tokyo. Being with Hideaki and Aiko was a life saver for me. Aiko knew exactly how I felt managing a baby and a three year old. She had the same experience in Manila. Hideaki knew of the emptiness of not having your loved one. He was able to console Sam, and he and his son, Yosuka, played together. He insisted that Sam learn Japanese, and over the six months I was there, he became fluent in Japanese. As I became calmer, our baby, John William, became less demanding. I knew he was reacting to my tension. Then you came to Tokyo for Christmas, and you were all screwed up. I had longed for a loving husband that had left me and what did I get? I got an emotional cripple. You chose to put yourself in a hell hole when the Army was going to send you to Camp Rucker, Alabama. That unit was retired in March, 1953, and you could have had an early discharge. You would have had none of those horrible experiences. You could have had your year with Sam and not given it to Hideaki. You can see, Charles, I have a lot of questions of why would you do that. Even your internship was harder than it needed to be. You were going to get enough experience in surgery equivalent to a third year resident and didn't consider what that pressure did to me and our relationship. You knew I wanted to start our family, and you went along with your goals and made me a victim of wanting to have children that you fathered. As you can see, I am frustrated and angry over the choices you have made. As I see it, you didn't consider me at all."

At first, Charles was dumbfounded. As she proceeded, he felt angry and wanted to interrupt. Finally, he began to see how his decisions were not the best for them. He began to think about why he was so driven. He looked at his life and realized he had always driven himself to be the best. He never thought of the consequences. He knew he must think more about this, but now he must do something to help Lillian.

He started off by saying that he could see how selfish he had been. He said, "I, not only hurt you, but also I exposed myself to the horror of war again. I realized when I came to Tokyo that Christmas how much damage I had imposed on myself. I must do something with this over achieving self. It seems to drive me. I want to be loving to you. I want to be aware of what I do and how it will affect you and my family. When I was trying to think how I was to answer you, my first thought was to say I love you. I felt that this was unfair, and it could disarm you before I acknowledged what you had said was true. I must be confronted. Now, I don't have to be fair. I can say with all of my heart. I love you and my family." With this he hugged her and kissed her tenderly. All of the pains were disappearing.

Lillian wanted him to tell her what he had experienced. He said, "Lillian, there were some light moments for me during that period, but they were surrounded with so much death and despair that I can't talk about them without all of the other flooding in. I think, as I get away from it, I will eventually talk to you about it. Right now, I just want to heal all of the things that might keep us apart." They decided that they had said enough for now. Their conversation had been very intense, and they had sleeping boys that did not need to be disturbed. Coming out of this intensity, they became aware that their airplane was landing in Rochester. They hurriedly waked the boys and left the plane. Much to their surprise, Dr. Holman and his wife met the plane.

As they approached the waiting area, Dr. Holman and his wife rushed to greet them. He said, "Charles and Lillian, I want you to meet Jane, my wife. Lillian, I have heard so much about you that I feel that I know you." This warm greeting was a surprise to Lillian. Charles had not discussed his relationship with Ted.

Dr. Ted Holman had spent a month at the Mash unit with Charles and his group of doctors. They became friends. Ted was twice Charles' age, but age was not a barrier to them. Charles had talked to Ted about how he felt about surgery. He said, "I first thought that surgery was a technique to be mastered, and I did everything to master it. As I went along with this idea, I was discovering techniques that I was learning were not working like I felt they should. Also, I began to realize that these techniques for some conditions didn't work at all." Ted was at first surprised to hear this from a young doctor, and he started to take a second look at Charles. As they talked further, he realized he was talking to a thinking doctor. It was then he decided that he wanted Charles to come to the Mayo Clinic and work with him. When his month was up, he told Charles he wanted him to consider coming to the clinic and working with him. He emphasized the "with". This was what he told Lillian when she asked why Ted was so friendly. They had written many letters to each other.

When Charles decided to apply to the Mayo Clinic, he asked Ted to find a real estate agent that would be able to help locate a house for his family. He said he wanted a five bedroom home with five bathrooms.

He wanted a large back yard, and he was looking at a price range of $300,000. Furthermore, he could go higher, if necessary. This astounded Ted, as he had no idea that Charles had that much money. By 1953, his investments with Akihiko and Hideaki were valued in the millions. His Japanese brothers were among the new wealth of Japan. So when they arrived in Rochester, Lillian had a choice of several large homes. When she expressed surprise about the size of these houses, Charles reminded her that she had told him that there were still two girls to come into their family. Also, they needed a room and a private bath for his mother. Lillian laughed, and they had fun picking out their home. As it turned out, the houses they looked at were the type of houses in which the Mayo staff lived. Charles and Lillian were to live in Ted and Jane's neighborhood. Lillian was to become a close friend of Jane.

CHAPTER 26

By the 15th of June, 1953, Charles started his first year at the Mayo Clinic. Ted got him assigned to his unit. At this time, Ted was doing surgery at Saint Mary's Hospital. The Mayo Clinic office buildings were located in downtown Rochester. They were bound on the east by Broadway Avenue, on the south by fourth Street SW and on the north by Methodist Hospital and 2nd Street SW. Saint Mary's Hospital was one mile west on 4th Street SW.

Charles had been instructed to meet his staff doctor at the doctor's private lounge. There he would meet Dr. Holman and his first assistant (a third year fellow). He was early and was waiting when they arrived. Ted greeted Charles using his first name and Charles responded, "Good morning, Ted." The third year fellow had hardly noticed Charles at that moment, but the calling of his staff doctor by his first name startled him. He expected a rebuke but none came. Nothing else was said, and they started their rounds. Charles had come very early and had found out who and where Dr. Holman's patients were and had familiarized himself about their problems. Ted was not surprised that he had done this. His first assistant was puzzled, and somewhat angry. When Dr. Holman left, the first assistant made it clear to Charles that he was a first year fellow and that he was to take orders from him. Charles had expected this and said nothing. He thought to himself, now I know how a war veteran feels when he meets his upper classman at West Point. Here, he was a tested warrior, and now, he was being commanded by an adolescent.

As the days passed, his first assistant, Jack Sharp, became aware of his value as a second assistant. He could depend upon his judgment, and he was extremely helpful in surgery. Charles gave him two more hands. He could relax and enjoy his duties because he didn't have to teach or watch out for errors with Charles. When he would talk with his peers, he found himself saying, "You had better watch out about this Bettendorf guy because he will probably know more than you do." They thought he was joking, but by the time Charles was through his second three months, they knew it was no joke.

Lillian was happy with her new home. She had help with the children, and life was easier. The nanny she found was a very capable, hardworking, Swedish descent girl, who talked with a Swedish accent. When Charles told her that many of the staff workers were of Swedish origin, she thought no wonder the clinic was so efficient. Lillian found that her neighbors were very friendly. Jane introduced her to her friends. All of these women's husbands were staff doctors. This made no difference. Lillian captivated them, and they were fascinated by her experiences. When they learned that she had taught the Japanese language and that Sam spoke fluent Japanese, to say "surprised" would be an understatement. Some of them wanted to start a Japanese language class, but Lillian was not interested.

It so happened that the clinic was getting a fairly large number of wealthy Japanese patients. There was a language problem. Ted was at a staff meeting when this problem was brought up. He quickly told them about the Bettendorf family. They asked him to approach the Bettendorfs about whether they would be willing to help them with this problem. The Bettendorfs didn't want to engage into any activities that would affect the time they had for themselves. As more Japanese came, the problem became more acute. Lillian was pregnant, and she was not able to be an interpreter.

Aiko's youngest daughter, Asami, wanted to study in the United States. They were reluctant to let her go. Akemi was too busy to take on the responsibility of her sister. When Lillian wrote that the clinic was having trouble with not having a Japanese interpreter, Aiko wrote back wondering if Asami would be a prospect for the job. Lillian thought that it was a great idea and told Charles to find out if the clinic was interested. Their first question was whether she was fluent in English. He said, "Yes, Lillian had taught her." So, in a few weeks, Asami arrived and was employed by the clinic. Her one condition was that she be allowed to study the Mayo Clinic business model. It took a year and a half for her to complete this task. She talked repeatedly about her father's company in Japan. Finally, one of her bosses looked up this company. He found that it was a large international company. The owners were Okada, Fugimaki and Bettendorf. They were surprised and impressed.

In the beginning, she lived with the Bettendorfs, but like her sister, she wanted her own apartment. Asami was a confident and directed young lady. She adored her only father as she called him. He had given her love and caring that her natural father was never willing to do. All she ever got from him was terror. It was the love Hideaki gave her that turned her into the woman she was today. Her directed behavior enabled her to finish her period of exploring the Mayo Clinic business model in a year and a half. She knew that she needed more academic study of business to be of help to her father and his company. She applied to Harvard Business School.

By the fall of 1959, she entered Harvard. She worked very hard and found that she was competing with a young Japanese student that was on a business fellowship from Tokyo University. When the end of the first year ended, they were tied for first place academically. All during that year they were aware of their competition.

It was Christmas time, and everyone had left for home. Asami had ruled out going to Japan or Minnesota. She wanted to spend the holidays doing research on how to acquire large corporations.

Her father had written they were prepared to make acquisitions of large companies. He wanted her to do research on the problems and solutions involved with this effort. She knew that her competitor, Kazuki Honami, who also was staying at the University over the holidays, had done advanced studies in problems of acquisitions of large corporations. To his surprise, she came to him and asked him to help her with this problem. They started working together and found it was comforting to share and explore information about a real acquisition.

Kazuki was surprised to find that this company sounded much like the company his father owned. He wrote home and asked his father if he was trying to sell his company. The answer that came back was, "How did you know this as it was a secret between him and the acquiring company? Your question indicates that information has gotten out." He was very upset. When Kazuki told Asami about this, they both laughed. They were pleased that both parties had been so honorable with each other. Both wrote their respective parents and explained, what had happened. Kazuki offered to stop helping Asami. Neither parent would hear of it. When they finished their work, they were no longer competitors but had become lovers. When they finished their graduate course in business administration, they left together and returned to Japan. Asami insisted that they stop in Rochester, Minnesota. She wanted him to meet Lillian and Charles. When she introduced Kazuki to Lillian and Charles, he was surprised when they responded in perfect Japanese and did all of the proper gestures that would have been done if they were Japanese. She told Kazuki she had adopted them as her aunt and uncle, and he was to treat them with the respect they deserved. She said, "Lillian gave her hope, and Charles gave her a father." After a few days, they left for Tokyo. They were planning to get married in the summer, when Charles and Lillian would be there. They were brought into the company and were in charge of acquisitions.

CHAPTER 27

It was time to bring Leah to live with them. She was very happy to be with them. Lillian introduced her to all of her friends. Leah was only 55 and was an attractive woman. Soon she was dating a staff doctor, who had lost his wife several years ago. Leah, with the help of Lillian, had become a more assertive person. The mixture of her old passive self and her new assertive self made her personality attractively different. Her doctor friend became more interested in her than she was in him. Her experience with Charles' father had been too scarring for her to consider another marriage. He was going to have to be patient with her.

When Asami began writing about how wonderful the clinic was Akihiko and Hideaki thought it would be a good idea to have their annual business meeting with Charles at Rochester. At the same time, they could get their annual physical examinations. It was decided that the best time to come to Rochester was in late May. Usually after the 15th of May, the snow was melted, and the short spring began. Charles prepared for Akihiko and Hideaki's families by renting two luxurious apartments and hired chauffer driven cars, so they could get around easily. The apartment building had a large conference room, so everything could go smoothly. The day of arrival came, and the three families were excited to be together. For a few days, little business was done. Charles had set up their examinations, and they were seen by the top physicians of the clinic. They were impressed by their competency. All of their physicians told them what a fine surgeon Charles was. When it was time for them to leave, they said, "This is the place we will have future meetings."

Sam and his buddy, Yosuka were and will be friends for life. Lillian, Ayame, and Aiko did many things together. Lillian's new friends were impressed with Aiko and Ayame. Their English was perfect, and they were very interested to find out how Lillian and they met.

Ayame was the first one to talk. She said, "Aiko and I were from different kinds of families. My parents were professors at the Tokyo Imperial University. Their teachings were supervised by a centrally controlled educational system. At that time, it was dominated by militarism. Girls had limited education, as they were expected to marry and have children for the Emperor and country. Because I was connected with the University through my parent's work, I met many young male students. It was there I met Akihiko. He was a handsome, young man, who was only interested in his studies. He had come from a poor farm family and was at the University on a scholarship. His scholarship was sponsored by the military. He was being trained to be fluent in English, as they were already planning to attack America. The military wanted English speaking interrogators, as they expected to conquer the United States. My parents were teaching English, so Akihiko was known to them. He was a very promising student, and my father would invite him to our home. They would discuss languages. Akihiko wanted to study Japanese language, and my father agreed to teach him privately. The military would not have approved of this. The scholarship only paid for his tuition, and he had no living expenses. Akihiko had to work at anything he could find in order to stay in school. I noticed that he was very thin and on two occasions, he fainted while he was studying with my father. My father asked him if he was getting enough to eat as he looked as if he was starving. He quickly replied that he was. We didn't believe him. As he was leaving one day, my father asked him if he could stay and help him with some outside work he had to do. He quickly agreed. It was late when they finished, and my father insisted that he stay for supper. My father said that he had much work to do around the house, and he needed a worker. He continued and said, "I have no money to pay you, but I can give you room and board for your work." He asked Akihiko if he was interested. He was. This led to our falling in love, and we were married. At graduation he was assigned to an infantry division, but he worked mainly in Tokyo. During the thirties, we had two girls, Chie (meaning wisdom) and Chiase (meaning one thousand mornings). They were born in 1933 and 1935. They are now 23 and 25. When the war broke out, Akihiko was sent to the Philippines and stayed there until the war was over. He was captured by Charles and returned to Japan when the war was over. The girls and I were in the Tokyo fire storm and by a miracle, escaped. My parents died in the flames. The girls and I went to Kyoto to live with relatives. That is where Charles and Akihiko found us. Over the last two years, the girls have married and their husband work for our companies." It amazed the women to hear this story.

Aiko's story was about two husbands. Her first husband and the danger she endured gave a new perspective of how the war time Japanese lived and suffered. Her description of how her first husband treated her angered them. Her determination to survive, and her finding Lillian was heart rendering.

They could easily see why Lillian and Aiko were so closely bound to each other. They left the meeting feeling all humans are connected and have the same problems and fears. They talked how governments can lead their citizens into serious problems, and it could destroy many innocent lives. All of Lillian's friends were looking forward to Aiko and Ayame's return. As the visit wound down Ayame, Aiko, and Lillian said a painful goodbye, but this time they had a future.

CHAPTER 28

In June, 1954, Charles was entering his second year at the Mayo Clinic. By now the surgical stuff realized that he was a peer with them. He was a first assistant in all of his surgical procedures. In severe cases, he was asked by many staff men to assist.

Charles felt that now was the time to begin research on problems of surgery. He was interested in trauma involving the chest and the abdomen. He was considering shock. He wanted to know what the factors were that occur when shock becomes irreversible. If he could find the factors causing this shock, he might be able to modify them and recover the patient. In Korea, he had watched young soldiers go into irreversible shock, and he was completely helpless to save them. One case had been on his mind repeatedly and reminded him of the despair he felt as he watched this young soldier slip away.

This soldier had come in with a groin wound involving the femoral artery. The artery had partially retracted into the abdomen, and the aid man had partially controlled the bleeding. He was in beginning shock when he arrived. Charles knew he must get hold of the retracting artery immediately. Blood was being pumped into the soldier, but he was bleeding faster than the replacement. He was talking to Charles asking him to please save his life. He kept saying, "Doc, it's only a leg wound." Slowly he sank into irreversible shock, and his last faint words were "save me". Reliving this made Charles' decision. He would study irreversible shock. He asked Ted if he was interested in this problem. Ted said, "Are you remembering that soldier that we lost to shock?" "Yes, and I can't get his face out of my mind." replied Charles. Ted said, "I am not interested in that research, but I will help you get started." The funding for this project was not available. Charles decided to fund it himself. This project would last for over a year and a half.

He was primarily interested in loss of blood volume shock, but he did study anaphylactic shock and bacterial shock. It seemed to him that the integrity of the capillaries and pooling of the blood might be a common factor. As he went along, he published his findings. There was little interest in his work.

He was very careful in how he used his time. Lillian was very alert to his tendency to over involve himself in his work and insisted that he give his family their share of his time. Towards the end of 1954, Lillian was pregnant. The baby girl was born on the 12th of August, 1955. Their house was filling up.

Leah continued to date Dr. James Williams. They had a good relationship, but Leah didn't want marriage. In October of 1955, she developed a lump in her right breast. It frightened her, and she started to withdraw from the family and James. Lillian was the one most sensitive to this. She kept asking Leah what was the matter. All she got was the old passive personality she had worked so hard to get Leah to abandon. This change made her even more aware that something bad must be happening to her mother-in-law. She talked to Charles about her concerns. He had no idea what might be wrong. Finally, Lillian cornered Leah and would not let her escape. Leah burst out crying and said she had found a lump in her right breast. She was afraid she had cancer and that she was going to die just like her husband. Lillian immediately called Charles, and Leah was seen that day by the service that specialized in breast cancer.

It so happened that Dr. Williams was one of the leading doctors in that division. When he heard who the patient was that had come to their service, he left immediately to be by her side. He gave to Leah the caring concern for which she had always longed. Something inside her changed in her feelings towards James. James was again going through his loss of his first wife. As he looked at Leah, he said to himself, "I will not let this happen to me again. I lost my first wife to breast cancer, and I will not lose Leah." When his first wife died, he changed his interest in medicine to breast cancer.

The breast biopsy showed grade four cellular pathology. Surgery was performed. It was a radical mastectomy with an axillary lymph node dissection. Her nodes were free of cancer. James had assisted, and he was in constant attendance. In fact, he took leave from his work to be with her. This devotion convinced Leah that she wanted to live with James the rest of her life. She told him that she loved him and had for a long time. She had been afraid to be married again. His caring for her had given her courage to want to be with him the rest of her life. She asked James if the loss of her breast affected his feeling for her. He said, "I didn't fall in love with your breast." As soon as she recovered, they were married. Charles was the best man, and Lillian was the matron of honor.

When Leah moved into her new home, it was her grandchildren that missed her the most. The last year of Charles' training was uneventful. Lillian was beginning to think that maybe three children were enough. She was tired of diapers and nursing a new baby. She was realizing that the children were taking more and more time away from her relationship with Charles. She said to Charles, "I think I am doing what I accused you of. I am spending too much time with the children and not enough with you. I am thinking that three children are enough, and I hope you will agree." Charles was excited and said, "I have longed for more time with you." All of this talk was for naught. Lillian was pregnant six months later. She said to Charles, "I wore a diaphragm every time. I don't see how it happened."

In June, 1955, Akemi and Daniel wrote Charles. Daniel was finishing his internship at Vanderbilt University, and he wanted to come to the Mayo Clinic for his internal medicine residency. He asked Charles if he could recommend him and help him get an acceptance. He sent his grades from Vanderbilt and a letter of his work as an intern. Both of these documents gave high marks for Daniel.

Charles wrote he would help, but he felt that Daniel's performances would be enough to get him an appointment. He was accepted for June, 1955. So Akemi and Lillian were reunited. They helped them get settled and were pleased to meet, for the first time, their little boy. Aiko had written about the baby, and in their visit Hideaki was talking about his latest grandson.

CHAPTER 29

Now Charles was ending his fellowship at the Mayo Clinic. He had only two more months, and they would be at another crossroads in their life. Two families were talking about them coming to live near them. Hideaki and Akihiko wanted them to come and help them run their businesses. They said, "We will build you a hospital, and you will have no problem practicing in Japan." Aiko wrote Lillian and said the same things. Lillian's family wanted them to come to Athens, Georgia. They said, "We have a fine hospital, and after all, we are family." The Mayo Clinic offered Charles a staff position and Ted and Jane wanted them to stay. All of these opportunities were very inviting to them.

Charles and Lillian had two months to make up their minds. They decided that they would write down the advantages of each opportunity and try to decide from that. When they talked to the children, Sam wanted to go to Japan, so he could be with his other father and Yosuka. The other children were too young to have an opinion. Lillian liked the idea of being around Aiko. She remembered how much she helped her when Charles was in Korea. Charles would like to be around Hideaki and Akihiko. He enjoyed their businesses and would like to contribute to them. The drag to these ideas was that they would be a long way from Leah and Lillian's family.

The Mayo Clinic was a good place to live, and they had a fine home and many friends. Charles had a good position offer, and they could be happy here. Strangely, going back to Athens didn't seem as appealing as it had in the past. They had seen Lillian's family very few times during their training period, and Sam had not connected with his cousins. Charles wanted to have some period of time with his Japanese friends, but he didn't want to settle there for their permanent address. They decided that they would sleep on it and see if anything crystallized out.

By the end of May, they decided that they would stay at the Mayo Clinic if certain conditions could be met. They wanted to spend every summer in Japan. This was a problem with the clinic as their busiest season was the summer. The committee for the staff debated this request. The final vote for his request was a no. None of the members would budge from their vote. Charles and Lillian were planning to leave in June and move to Athens, Georgia. Charles felt that he could go to Japan any time he wanted if he was in practice for himself. They packed up and left on June 15, 1956. Ted was furious with the committee, and he said so.

Two months after they left, all of his publications on shock suddenly became of interest to a large number of investigators. They were writing to the clinic requesting for Charles to come and lecture to their staff and examine their work on shock. Ted was thrilled and made his disgust known to the committee, who had rejected his friend. The committee reconvened to discuss the new information. They unanimously decided to write Charles and tell him they had made a mistake and ask if he would reconsider and come back to the clinic. They decided that their first decision was based on finances and not on the academic skills that he offered the clinic. Ted added a note to this letter and said, "They had their chance and flubbed it. Do what is best for you."

By this time, they had settled down in Athens, and the children were enjoying their cousins. When Sam was told that they would go to Japan every summer, the move was okay with him. Lillian had reconnected with her old friends and was content. Charles wrote back thanking them for their letter, but he was too settled to consider returning to the clinic. Now, Charles and Lillian had taken a new path in their lives. Their fourth child, a baby girl, had been born on July 8, 1956, and Lillian's planned family was complete. Charles would be 31 in September, and Lillian was 32 in February. They felt that their lives would be uncomplicated, as Charles would be developing his practice, and Lillian with his help would raise their family. This was true for a while.

Changes in their community and the United States were beginning to affect them. The civil rights movement was advocating desegregation of schools. Georgia was against integration of schools. Charles was an active supporter for civil rights. This caused problems in Lillian's family and in the community. His patients began to boycott him, and there was talk against him and Lillian. When this happened, the four brothers changed sides and openly supported Charles and his family. Charles and Lillian talked with Lillian's family and said they were leaving. They didn't want to fight another battle. They were tired of angry people that could not debate their ideas. They only wanted to fight irrationally.

Charles wrote Ted at the clinic and told him of the problems in Georgia. He asked if the offer was still available at the clinic. When Ted took the letter to the staff committee, they said, "We are not making the same mistake twice." Immediately, a warm telegram was sent welcoming him back with his conditions being acceptable. Charles had not been able to sell his home, and all they had to do was to move back and be with their old friends. Lillian's family understood and had mixed feelings about their living. With Charles gone, anger against their family stopped, and they were grateful for that. To lose Lillian and all was difficult to accept. Bill was so upset that he decided he would go into politics.

Because of their investments in Japan, Lillian's parents were independently wealthy. Dan and Lucy could choose any direction they wanted, and this whole desegregation problem angered them. They decided that they hated prejudice, and each was going to see what they could do to change things. The first thing they thought they must do is not let any of their efforts get polarized. People must be able to have a rational dialogue. They would have a long way to go.

The move back to Mayo was relatively easy. Sam didn't miss much school and easily caught up. All of the neighbors were delighted to have them back, and it was particularly so with Jane and Ted. The value of his work was now widely accepted as basic research in shock and its management. The clinic was anxious for him to continue in this work. Amazingly, Akihiko and Hideaki were delighted to have him back at Mayo's. They liked Rochester so well that they built a small compound for both families to use. They intended to visit frequently. They still expected for Charles and Lillian to come to Japan in the summer. Summer finally came and the family was off to Tokyo.

CHAPTER 30

The reason why they wanted Charles to be in Japan for a period of time was because he had the ability to sense opportunities that were in an early stage of development. In other words, his thinking projected into the future with remarkable accuracy. Quite early he sensed that Japan, in order to develop industrially, would have to develop quality goods and not cheap goods. Before the war, Japan was known for producing only cheap goods. He told his partners they must look for companies that were quality oriented, and they must insist that all of their products were of highest quality. He said, "Japan has the advantage of cheap labor. We must take advantage of this and gain market share." Their success based on cheap labor would eventually be lost as their country prospered. They partly agreed. Because he had led them well in the past, they implemented his ideas. Things went slowly for a while. Profits were flat. Charles insisted that they continue. Slowly they began to see changes. There was an increase in demand for their quality products. They started to be able to demand higher prices for their products. It seemed that Charles was getting it right.

Lillian and her group were involved with cultural issues. One thing they felt was important was that their children should be bilingual. Each should speak Japanese and English well. This would be a tradition of their children and their grandchildren. Lillian had always been involved in feeding the poor, and she wanted her group to develop a charitable organization that would help the poor. Her motto was "don't just feed them, teach them. We help you, so you can help yourself." The women liked this idea, and a charity was begun.

When Tokyo's medical society heard a Mayo doctor, who did all of that work on shock, was in town, they immediately formed a committee to approach him. They wanted him to attend their meetings and to give lectures. Charles was reluctant to do this. He wanted to be with his friends and help them in their projects. They kept insisting, but to no avail. Finally, they asked the family doctors of Akihiko and Hideaki to ask if they would persuade their friend to at least come to one of their meetings. The three talked it over and decided that it would be a good idea for Charles to be active in the medical society of Tokyo. The first meeting was fun for Charles. He talked fluent Japanese, and this was very pleasing to his audience. He talked briefly about his current work on shock and indicated that his studies were beginning to consider the molecular level of the healing of traumatized tissue. This intrigued his audience.

When they learned that he was coming yearly to Tokyo for three months, they without his knowledge elected him as an honorary member of their society with all of the privileges. They knew of his skills and wanted him to be available to perform surgery at their hospitals.

This was going to cause a problem as the practice of medicine in Japan required that the person be a resident in good standing and a graduate of an accredited medical school. It was the residency clause that created the problem. Again, a committee was formed with the task of finding out if a solution was possible. They went first to the executive branch of the government, and were referred to the diplomatic branch. They addressed their applicant as Dr. Charles Bettendorf. The diplomats listened politely and refused the request. As the committee was leaving, muttering loudly that they couldn't understand how the government could be so uncompromising. Here for the first time they had an excellent doctor, who could speak fluent Japanese and who understood Japanese customs so well, that to hear him talk was a great pleasure. One of the officials hearing "Japanese customs so well" stopped them. He asked, "Is this man the Charles Bettendorf that had been in MacArthur's headquarters?" They said, "We don't know, but we could call him and see." The diplomat was anxious for an answer and let them use his phone. They called the headquarters of Charles' company and asked to speak to Charles. They said it was important and that he should be interrupted. They were getting nowhere. The diplomat took the phone and identified his position. He insisted that they interrupt his conference.

The secretary was alarmed and went immediately to the meeting and told Charles that the diplomatic service was demanding to talk with him. He felt some anxiety about this message and picked up the phone. The diplomat was very polite and said, "A committee from the Tokyo Medical Society is in my office requesting an honorary citizenship for you. They said it was necessary for you to have this in order to do an instructive surgical procedure. The diplomatic corp has refused this request, but I, Kami Fugiyama, was intrigued by their comments about …" Charles interrupted with an excited voice, "Kami, is it you?" Kami said, "It is me!" They both began talking rapidly with each other. At a pause, Kami told the rest of the diplomats with whom he was speaking. They all remembered Charles well. One older person recalled how he had helped get the return of Aiko Yamamoto. All were excited that he was back in Japan. During all of this excitement, the doctors were standing amazed. Eventually, Kami related how important Charles had been during the MacArthur years in helping them communicate with his staff. The diplomat committee reconvened and unanimously agreed that Charles should have an honorary citizenship and he should specifically have the right to do surgery in Japan. The medical committee was very impressed by what had transpired, and they were excited about his being able to do surgery. Before Kami hung up, he insisted that Charles come to their offices and meet old friends. Charles was just as excited as they were and said, "I will come soon."

All of these happenings opened many avenues for Charles, and he started talking to himself. He said, "I must not overload myself and neglect my families." He meant his family and his brothers' families as his main reason for being there was them and their businesses.

When Lillian heard about what had happened, she told Charles she and the other wives were developing charity ideas. One of the ideas was forming a hospital for the many employees of their companies. She said that they could pattern the health care after the Kaiser Company's health care program. While she was telling Charles this, the other wives were telling their husbands the same thing. In the next meeting, this matter was brought up, and all agreed that it fit well with the developing corporate ideas in Japan. It was decided that they would appoint Lillian to explore how this Kaiser plan worked, and they would discuss it over the next year. They would be able to finalize it when they met in May for their annual medical visits at the Mayo Clinic. This meant that Charles and Lillian would leave a week early, so Lillian would have time to visit the Kaiser Foundation before flying to Rochester.

On the flight home, Charles found himself in deep thought. He was telling himself that he had not really paid much attention to what was happening in the world. His life time had been during three presidents. Roosevelt had been president through most of World War II. He made many decisions during the depression that were controversial. His containment policies and Japan's expansion demands led to conflict with Japan. His concern about the conquests of Germany led to war with Germany. All of these forces put him (Charles) on a boat in November, 1944 -- a scared nineteen year old. The atomic bomb was dropped and for a while the United States had a unique position of power. Through Russian espionage and betrayal, they had an atomic bomb in 1949. Many bombs were exploded, and it rained radioactive materials across the globe. The cold war was dominating the world and holding it hostage.

Harry Truman became president on April 12, 1945 (Roosevelt died). Charles, at that time, was in Australia in O.C.S. Lillian was in his life. The Korean War came, and when Eisenhower was elected, an armistice was signed. There was much posturing between Russia and the United States, but no serious events occurred until Spudnik happened, and a new area of conflict appeared.

In many ways, Charles again was thinking that government could be dangerous to people's lives. He wondered the whole flight back how he could address this problem.

Lillian and the children had slept most of the flight over the Pacific and were rested. Charles was exhausted. When they landed in San Francisco, they went immediately to a hotel. Lillian was off to the Kaiser Foundations, and Charles went to bed. Ingrid, the nanny, was instructed to keep the children busy and to let Charles sleep. The first two stages of sleep (about one-and-one-half hours each) were dreamless. In the fourth hour of sleep, he began to dream about the thoughts he had had on the plane. The idea that the government was dangerous to their citizens was disturbing to him. As he explored this idea, he found himself remembering articles he had read about Senator Chavez of New Mexico. He was championing the men of Bataan. He claimed they had fought well, and the country had failed them. The government's position expressed by Henry Stimson, Department of Army, was that our men had not fought well as a group and did not deserve the praise that the Senator was promoting. It took some time before the public was allowed, not by the government, but by newspaper reports, to know about the cruelty of the Japanese soldiers, and how well the Americans had fought on Bataan. The reason why the government had censored information about Bataan was that they knew Americans would be so incensed that they would insist that attacking Japan was the first priority. This would make fighting Germany of secondary importance. Churchill and Roosevelt wanted Germany to have first priority. So the truth was censored and distorted.

Americans and their Filipino soldiers had fought hard without adequate supplies and were starving when they did surrender. Actually, it was General Wainwright, who ordered them to surrender. It was the newspapers that uncovered the death march even though the government had known about it months before. He wondered why governments would deceive their citizens. He had just come back from Japan, and they were openly discussing how their government had betrayed them.

His thoughts shifted to Bill, his brother-in-law. He was upset by the behavior of his supposed friends regarding the family's support of Charles' support for the integration of schools. His idea was that the fault resided with the government. Charles, at the time, was puzzled by this idea. He felt it was a cultural problem. Now, he was not so sure. This distrust of the government was so disturbing to him that he woke up and couldn't go back to sleep.

He heard the children murmuring in the next room and had a great idea. He wanted to quit thinking about the government. He felt the best way was to get out into San Francisco and enjoy its ambience. He particularly wanted to take the children to Camp Stoneman and visit the camp and go down to the pier where in November, 1944, he loaded on a barge to go overseas.

He left the two girls with Ingrid as they were too young for this adventure. He and the two boys drove to Camp Stoneman. It wasn't the same place. It seemed almost abandoned. He was able to find the dock, but he couldn't find his old barrack. While standing on the pier, he was flooded by memories of his fears and his inability to focus his mind. He had not really seen much of the trip to San Francisco. He said to his boys, "Let's get a boat and go down the Bay to San Francisco." He was able to turn in his car and find a boat that would take them down the Bay to the boat docks of San Francisco.

So off they went. This time, he saw the beauty of his surroundings. The Bay was calm, and they deliberately went very slowly. It was late evening when they arrived at the boat docks. The city was all lit up, and it was so different. They caught a cab and went to their hotel. Lillian answered the door and was concerned as she had no idea where they had been. The boys were very excited and told her all about how Dad had gone to war.

As they usually did when they had gone different paths, they sat down and talked about their experiences and their thoughts of the day. Lillian was pleased about her talks with the staff of the Kaiser Health Program. She felt that their structure needed a careful analysis and didn't feel qualified to evaluate it. She wanted to hire a consultant to help explore this structure. She asked Charles where she would find such a person. Charles suggested she call the clinic administration division and see if they could tell her if such a person was available in San Francisco. Since it was late, she was going to call the first thing in the morning.

Charles started talking about his day, but mostly about the thoughts he was having. He said, "My thoughts are disturbing to me. I have always trusted my government to do the right thing." He knew that it wasn't perfect, but he had felt that it was trustworthy. He was now questioning this. He was feeling betrayed by his government. He felt that the bottom line to all of his wondering was that the government didn't trust its citizens. They seemed to feel that on complex issues the less the public knew the better. His experiences in Japan convinced him that when a government is open, then the citizens are served best. He felt that the only way to get an open government was to have open citizens. He told Lillian that from now on he was going to be open with his thoughts.

He was going to take chances that openness brought. Regardless of the circumstances, he was going to speak out when he felt something was wrong. He would not take the safe course of silence, which was agreeing by silence with what he knew was wrong. The silence of Europe when Hitler was rampaging only led to a horrific war. The silence about the rape of Nanking only led to the horrors of the Pacific war.

Lillian was surprised by the intensity of his feelings. She was silent for a while thinking over what he had said. She was remembering times when her friends had made ethnic slurs, and she had felt repulsed. She had said nothing. She thought if she had real friends, they would accept her objections to their slurs. If they took offense and were angry with her objection, she would brand that cow at the right time. She smiled at the spontaneity of this saying. She remembered Sam Petrie using this statement.

After their talks, the whole family went to dinner and then to an early bed. They were still overcoming jet lag. Charles was going to use his free time in San Francisco to explore all of the city with his boys. Ingrid entertained the girls, and Lillian found her consultant and had a very successful experience. She mailed all of her findings to Aiko and Ayame. They would communicate about these reports over the next few months.

Charles was glad to get back to the business of the clinic and his research. He communicated with Hideaki and Akihiko regarding opportunities he was thinking about as well as about their building of a hospital for the care of their employees. Since he had enjoyed being in Japan so much, he asked them to locate some land near them, so he could build a small complex for his family to use when they were living in Japan. He sent the plans he had designed for the complex. It surprised them how Japanese these plans looked. They said, "It is to be finished and completed when he returns in the summer."

That winter was extremely cold. The snows started in September, and by October it would stay on the ground until the last days of May. In January and February, the temperature would barely reach zero at its warmest, and at night it dropped to minus 25 degrees. The children thrived in this weather, and Charles flooded a part of their back yard, so they could ice skate any time they wanted. Lillian and Charles were not used to this degree of coldness and adapted slowly. Christmas was really a white Christmas, and they all took sleigh rides. These were happy times, and Leah and her husband visited often. They were impressed by how much Leah had changed. She was no longer passive and was taking a leadership role in her activities. Charles gave all of this change to her husband. He was fascinated with Leah and could hardly stay away from her. She was the same about him.

CHAPTER 31

From 1958 to 1960, their lives each year were pretty much the same. The clinic noticed that Charles was developing a group of patients that would only see him. Many of these people used to come in the summer but finding that he was gone at that time led them to start coming in the winter. The hospital in Japan was built and was the state of the art. His standing in the Tokyo Medical Society increased in importance. He was asked to join several hospital staffs. He would only accept honorary positions. Honorary citizenship was given to all of his family. The diplomatic people asked him if he wanted a dual Japanese citizenship. He told them he would consult with his government. He was deeply honored by this. Eventually, he and his family did accept a dual citizenship.

Their businesses continued to grow, and they began acquiring stocks or part ownership of up and coming industries. For example, when Charles noticed that a small automobile was being sold in the United States, he investigated the company. The automobiles were priced well and were accepted by conservative people. He advised his group about buying into a company called Toyota.

His compound was completed as planned, and it pleased his family. Every summer when it came time to go to Japan, all family members were eager to hit the road.

In 1960 changes were beginning to happen. The Democratic Party was nominating a young Senator John Kennedy. He was Catholic, and the feeling was that a Catholic could not win. He was elected, and it was a generation change in the presidency. His energy and his campaign interested Charles. Early in his presidency many things worried Charles. The Bay of Pigs fiasco was troubling.

In 1959, Fidel Castro had driven out Batista and established a communistic government. Russia was supporting Fidel and transferring military equipment to Cuba. This led to the Cuban crisis. The fear of a nuclear war was a real possibility when Russia started shipping missiles to Cuba. Kennedy ordered the United States Navy to stop the Russian ship transporting the missiles to Cuba if they passed a certain point. This scared all Americans and the Kremlin. The Kremlin ordered Khrushev to order the ship to turn back. That stopped the threat of war but left scars.

When an atomic war seemed imminent, the government wanted its citizens to build bomb shelters. Not all people could afford to do this. In neighborhoods, where some built shelters and others didn't, conflicts became evident. Problems began when neighbors without shelters asked their neighbors with shelters to consider letting them use their shelter if there was an attack. Most of the shelters built accommodated only the family involved. If they told the neighbor there was no room for them, long time friends were lost. Solid caring neighborhoods vanished over night.

Charles realized this problem and refused to build a private bomb shelter. Instead, he started trying to get the city to identify such structures that would offer some protection. The cold war and a strong sense of insecurity were pervading the country. These forces seemed to climax in November, 1963.

When President Kennedy was visiting Dallas, he was shot and killed by a person, who had visited Russia and married a Russian woman. He had also visited Cuba. The CIA had at one time hired the mafia to assassinate Fidel Castro. This was stopped by Kennedy, but there was much speculation that Russia and/or Cuba were involved in the assassination of President Kennedy. This was very unsettling to all citizens, so much so that a commission headed by Supreme Court Justice Warren was formed to decide if there was a conspiracy. None was found, but people continued to wonder. Charles' concerns about government again entered his thoughts. When Johnson moved into the White House, he started passing civil rights laws that were radically changing cultural patterns. He became more involved in the Vietnam conflict. The draft was calling up young people that didn't feel that this war was in national interests. There was a teenage rebellion. Teenagers were being drafted to fight in Vietnam. Towards the end of his elected term, Johnson indicated he would not run. At that time there were more than 500,000 American troops in Vietnam. In 1968, Sam was nineteen and subjected to the draft. That summer when they were in Japan, Sam talked to Yosuka about what he intended to do.

CHAPTER 32

In a way Sam was recalling his life up to this point. He was in his second year of college, and he had joined the NROTC. He wrote a letter to Yosuka and said, "My early memories are around my father going to Korea. I can remember how upset I was, and how frightening it was. My mother was so upset. When I came with mother to Japan to be with you and Daddy Hideaki, I felt safe again. When my father returned, he was not like the father that left us. I think this has colored my life. I grew up wanting to be with Daddy Hideaki's family. I think I am more like my mother's brothers. I am more athletic and less intellectual than my father. I played all the sports that I could and had no trouble dating. My high school years were fun, but my best times were in the summers with you. All my plans of the future seem to be around getting back to Japan." He planned to get an exemption from the draft by signing a contract that would allow him to complete his NROTC training. After this, he would join the Navy for three years of duty. Yosuka was worried about his friend.

Charles and Lillian were furious about Vietnam. They didn't buy the containment policies of the government. They watched how France had tried to recolonize Vietnam after World War II. They admired how they had fought and won their freedom in North Vietnam. They did not feel that America should be involved in a civil war.

Johnson, using the issue of the Bay of Tonkin to build up the troops, upset them. Especially upsetting was discovering the second event did not occur. Charles was more and more suspect of his government. He was feeling very strongly that he must get involved in the political process. It was during this period that he received a letter from an old classmate. He was the oldest classmate in his class at Vanderbilt Medical School. Jim Davis was a very dedicated man, who wanted to do private practice in a small town. He chose Paris, Texas. He practiced there for 29 years and retired in 1980.

His letter started with him describing a robbery at his vacation cabin on the Red River. He and his wife were alone in a remote area. It was early one morning that a young man broke into their cabin, robbed them, and took their car. He had bound them, but Jim was able to escape and notify the sheriff. This young man was captured and brought to trial. He apparently came from a wealthy, prominent family in Dallas, Texas. He was represented by a very expensive lawyer. During the trial, he wrote a threatening letter to Jim and his wife. This young man felt they were the cause of his being captured, and he indicated that he would get revenge. Jim wanted the letter to be admitted as evidence of the violent nature of this person. The judge ruled that it was not material to the case, and it was not entered as evidence. The young man was convicted of robbery and this was objected to by the prosecuting attorney. He felt a stronger charge should be made. He was sentenced to serve 500 hours of public service. Jim went to the judge and protested the sentence saying that this man was a danger to himself and his wife. The judge curtly dismissed him. Three weeks later, this person broke into Jim's home and shot his wife, and in the ensuing gun fight, Jim shot and killed the young man.

Jim said he was furious with the judge and confronted him saying, "Because you would not listen to my fears, I have killed another human being, and my wife is seriously wounded." The judge was not interested in Jim's complaint. In response to this, Jim began a search of this judge's previous decisions.

This experience was not unusual for this judge. In a number of cases, seemingly improper decisions had been made. Jim pursued this and led an active campaign to get this judge removed. He was successful. Continuing he said, "I am writing this letter to you because I feel that I have not been attentive to politics, and this inattention has caused me serious consequences. I want to alert all of my friends that they should be more active in what is happening politically in their communities." This letter saddened Charles and moved him closer to wondering what he could do about his government.

Charles' concern about the Vietnam War led him to have a long talk with John William. He advised him to apply for either West Point or Annapolis. He wanted him to be well trained if he was going to have to go to war. John had always been close to his father. There was no sense of loss like his brother had experienced. His main interests were reading and studying. He was only fair in sports, but he was on the football team. He didn't date much in high school, and often wondered why. His looks came from his mother, but his intellect came from his father. Now his parents were talking about the Vietnam War. He didn't know how he felt so he decided to follow their feelings. Having heard all of the stories of the jungle from his father and Uncle Hideaki, he had no desire to be a part of that type of fighting. He decided to apply for Annapolis when he graduated from high school.

Charles pulled all the strings he had, and John was accepted at Annapolis. Charles and Lillian were seeing their family being torn apart. When John William left for Annapolis, they began to realize how their families must have felt when they left. The girls were fourteen and twelve. The empty bedrooms in their home reminded them of how lonely they were.

By the late 1970's, the final pathways were established by all of the families. Sam finished his service in the Navy. He had married a high school sweetheart, and they had started their family. They had a boy and a girl. They would eventually have four children. They added two boys. As soon as they could get organized, they left for Tokyo. Sam and Yosuka were to be trained to be the future managers of the company. He was happy to be with his other father and his closest friend, Yosuka. They both studied hard at their tasks and worked up through all parts of the corporation. They lived in the compounds that their parents had established, so they had both business and family contacts. Sam's wife, Mildred, had some difficulty adjusting. Sam insisted that she learn the Japanese language. This was very hard for her, but she finally succeeded. All of their children were bilingual. By 1990 Sam and Yosuka assumed complete control of the company. Akihiko's son-in-laws would represent his part of the company. They guided the company through recessions and the technical bubble. While many investors lost large sums of money during this time, they continued to succeed. By 2000 they felt they were at the top of their game.

John William decided to get a PhD in finance when he completed his obligations with the Navy. He organized for the parent company their mortgages banking division. He was first established in New York. After two years, he moved the organization to London, England. John had some of the personality of his maternal grandfather. He was conservative and more cerebral in his thinking processes. As he progressed in this manner, he started looking at his decision making process. He found that he would scrupulously study an investment, but he never did respond to his studies. It seemed that his action on a project came suddenly without the use of his studies. This puzzled him, and he wondered about it. Finally, he decided that he had two ways of approaching a problem, i.e. the intuitive response and the cognitive approach. He felt that his cognitive approach must feed into his unconscious, and there his decision took place. He started trusting his intuitions.

While in London, John met his wife to be. She was a tall, slim brunette with beautiful blue eyes. She was all business. John seemed to always find reasons to consult with her. She was aware of his interest, but she was of the new generation that felt a woman had other abilities besides being a house wife and a mother. She didn't want to date seriously as her career came first. She worked for a large insurance company. It took a long time for them to become serious. Agatha didn't object to having an affair with John, but that was all it could be. It went along this way for a while.

One day she began to notice she was becoming jealous concerning John. She noticed that women were attracted to John. He was very successful, and this added to their interest. She started to realize that this handsome man should belong to her alone. This attitude shocked her. She was acting like her mother, who had always preached to her "Find your man and stick to him." That meant, get married. She wondered how John might feel if she was to change their agreement. One night when they were relaxed and talking, she broached this subject. She started by saying she had noticed that she was becoming jealous of him. She said, "I am noticing that women are too interested in you."

John was amused. He replied, "I don't understand why you are jealous because you wanted an open arrangement. As you know, our relationship is not supposed to be permanent." She said, "That is just the point. I want to change our agreement." John was delighted with how the conversation was going. He said, "How do you want to change it?" Agatha had always been straight forward in expressing her thoughts. Now she felt clumsy and frightened by what she was about to propose. She was going to tell John she loved him and wanted to get married. Her words to him that expressed her contempt for women, who wanted to be a housewife and mother, came back to haunt her. John had accepted her as a lover. Would he want her as a wife? John could see her struggling. He was no longer amused. He sensed what she was struggling with and said, "Agatha, I have always loved you. I have wanted for us to be married ever since I met you. If you are feeling this way now, all I can think to say is, let's take action immediately." Agatha sighed and said, "Oh, John, you knew what I was thinking and said it for me. Yes, I love you, and I find I am like my mother. I want my man bound to me by marriage." The excitement of these commitments stimulated them sexually, and they had an intense experience that had never happened before. They knew now that when love is a part of sex, things are different.

They didn't wait. Agatha contacted her mother and started planning the wedding. All of John's family came. Agatha did not know this included his Japanese families. She was impressed by John's parents and how all were so closely connected. She exclaimed to John, "What a terrific family I am marrying into." They had a honeymoon in Japan, and this started her language experience. She had no problem with Japanese, as she already spoke German and French. Their sexual life became very passionate. It surprised them, but they had no desire to change it. Nine months and ten hours after their marriage, their first child was born. She was a baby girl. They would have three children. The other two were boys. With her help, his mortgage banking business became very sophisticated and successful. He would compete against large firms and win. He particularly liked to compete with Goldman Sacks and win. Since his company was tied with the larger company, he and Agatha would go frequently to Tokyo. Their children would be multilingual. Agatha liked her new family and admired his parents very much. The millennium promised good things for them.

CHAPTER 33

Lucy Aiko Bettendorf was much like her father. Very probably she was the smartest child of the family. Her physical appearance was a copy of her mother. Her good looks enabled her to be very popular in school with both the boys and the girls. She was not interested in dating as her interests were in science. In high school she won many awards. When it came time for college, she had the rare opportunity of being able to go to any university of her choice. Her thinking was directed to searching out a school that had the imminent professors, who were teaching in the fields in which she was interested. At that time it was the University of California at Berkley. She did her undergraduate studies there and went to Harvard Medical School. When she graduated she did a rotating internship at the University of Iowa. She applied for a fellowship at the Mayo Clinic and finished her fellowship there.

She immediately started working in her father's laboratory, and it was there she met her husband. He had just joined the Mayo staff, and when he met Lucy, he couldn't get her off his mind. He had to work hard to get Lucy to be interested in him. This was a new experience for him as he had always had an easy time getting women interested in him. Lucy found him attractive, but she realized that he had an easy acceptance from women. She didn't like his casual approach to her as if she was going to fall head over heels in love with him. Actually, it was he that fell head over heels in love with her. When he realized that his approach was not working, he felt desperate. He finally decided to talk with her father.

He went to Charles and declared himself as being hopelessly in love with his daughter. This was obvious to everyone. He asked Charles, "What can I do to convince Lucy I really love her?" Charles replied, "Lucy is a simple straight forward person. She only responds to like people. I think you are a fine doctor, but you are taken too much with yourself." This analysis shocked him. He went to his apartment and really looked at himself. He stopped pursuing Lucy as he felt his patterns of behavior were hurting his chances with her. His absence was disturbing to Lucy. She, too, began to think about her behavior. She realized she had never given Robert Strong any chance to be different with her.

They happened one day to run into each other at the staff's coffee room. They sat down and for the first time had a simple, straight forward talk. He told her he had been a self-centered person with her, and he realized what a fool he had been. He asked if it was possible for them to begin again. He said, "I know I am a different person, and I really do love you." She said, "I will be willing to start over." Their courtship was quite different this time, and in a short time, they were engaged. Lucy said, "I don't like long engagements." So, they married two months later. They had a good marriage and had four children, three girls and one boy.

They eventually developed their own laboratory and broke away from the clinic. They were supported by her family's corporation. Sam knew that their interest in molecular biology and stem cell research would at sometime be a viable industry. He wanted to be on the ground floor. He told Lucy that she would be limited in stem cell research in the United States because of the pro life objection to it. He convinced her to move to Japan, and he would set up a state of the art laboratory for her and her husband. They moved, and Robert and the children learned Japanese.

By the end of the 20th century, they had made significant progress and were looking forward to the new century.

Lillian Leah Bettendorf was an uncomplicated child. She took after her paternal grandmother. She and Leah were very close. She was an average student and had many friends. She was a kind and giving person. This did not mean that she would let people take advantage of her. Her grandmother, Leah, saw to that. She went to college and planned to be a nurse. After finishing her under graduate studies, she applied to Vanderbilt Nursing School as it offered a B.S. degree in nursing. There she met a medical student, Sam Thorn, and they fell in love. They married when they both graduated, and she helped support him during his internship. She encouraged him to apply for a Mayo fellowship. He was accepted, and they would live in Rochester all of their lives. Sam was expected to learn Japanese and this was no problem. They had two children, a boy and a girl.

Leah and her husband retired in 1965. They were born in the year 1898. At sixty-seven they started traveling. They saw most of the world. When they were in Rochester, they spent many hours with Lillian Leah's children. In 1985, Leah's husband developed chronic heart failure. He was incapacitated with this, and in 1987, at the age of 89 was unable to get out of his bed. Leah was in constant attendance. He died in his sleep on December 5, 1987. Leah did not collapse but took care of all of the arrangements. She continued with her activities and spent many hours with Lillian Leah's family. In 1990 at the age of 92, Leah died. Charles said it all when he said, "When my mother found her second marriage, she became the mother I longed for as a child."

Hideaki Fugimaki and Aiko were born in 1915. The Tokyo fire storm destroyed his first family. He and Aiko had one child, Yosuka. Hideaki was active in his company until 1990. At this time, all management was turned over to Yosuka and Sam. He considered Sam his son. He often wondered about how his life had changed over the years. In his early years, he was a fanatical militarist. He was a cruel warrior. When the emperor surrendered, he lost faith in his government. He remembered all of his comrades, who had died for a false god. The refreshment of meeting Charles and Lillian gave him a new path and a new God. Finding Aiko gave him a new family. His original enemy was now his best and only real friend. Each day he thanked God for giving love and meaning to his life. All through the 1990's, he lived a quiet life. At the turn of the century he was a spry eighty-five. He felt he would live for at least ten more years.

Aiko looked at her life and realized that her first marriage was without love or caring. Her first husband was a diehard militarist. He saw women having one purpose, and that was to have children and, preferably, boys. He was very disappointed having only girls. He didn't need Aiko for sex as he preferred Geisha women. When he was defending Manila, he made no effort to help them escape. He just didn't care. She saw Lillian and Charles in the same light as Hideaki. They saved her and helped her find a new, happy and loving life. Hideaki gave her a son and her girls, a father. She, too, thanks God for His blessings. In the nineties she enjoyed being with her family and Lillian when she was in Tokyo. When 2000 arrived she said, "I want to live as long as Hideaki. If he dies first, I will follow soon."

Yosuka Fugimaki was a love baby and manifested it all of his life. From his earliest memories, Sam was always there. They were born in the same year, and he always felt he was his brother. He didn't have the war experiences of Sam, and he was fearful for him during the Vietnam War. Sam's coming to Japan was one of the happiest days of Yosuka's life. He married and had two boys that were about the same age as Sam's boys. He hoped his boys and Sam's boys would have the same friendship that he had with Sam. In 1990, he and Sam were appointed co-Presidents of their families' company. They complimented each other, and the company prospered. They survived the tech bubble in excellent shape. He saw the twenty-first century as one that offered many opportunities.

Akemi Fujimaki was 16 years old when her mother married her real father. Her memories of her natural father were all painful. He obviously didn't love her and seemed to always resent the demands of just keeping her alive. When he was gone, she was free of fear. When he was home, she was constantly fearful. Her being with Hideaki changed her life. He helped her to be unafraid and by his encouragement she was able to go to the United States. Her finding of Daniel Petrie completed her life. They had two boys and two girls. The boys were very athletic and in high school were football stars. Their oldest was a quarterback and the youngest was a wide receiver. When the oldest boy was a senior and the youngest was a sophomore, they led Rochester High School to its only state championship.

Aiko's father-in-law, Sam Petrie, was at first afraid that their marriage would cause problems for their children, especially in Texas. This didn't happen. When the boys visited his ranch in the summer, they became so skillful in riding horses that they competed in the local rodeos. They were admired and liked by the local kids and were completely accepted.

The girls turned out to be very attractive young ladies. They were popular with the boys and the girls. Both were cheerleaders but not when their brothers were in high school. They married local men who they had dated in high school. The boys were influenced by their grandfather Hideaki and went to Japan to work with the company. They met Japanese girls and were married there.

As the company expanded, they took foreign positions and the youngest did finally settle in San Francisco. Their wives learned English and husbands of the girls learned Japanese. Akemi was born in 1932. She was 68 in 2000. Her husband retired that year, and they planned to spend more time with her parents. Sam Petrie and Jane died in 1997. Sam was 87.

Asami was born in 1934. She had the same experiences as Akemi with her father. She adored Hideaki and at an early age decided to be a business woman, so she could be with him. All her early life was dedicated with this purpose in mind. She got a PhD in finance from Harvard Business School. She brought important skills to the family business. Sam and Yosuka were very proud of her. She met and married a Japanese exchange student that she met at Harvard. He became a professor in economics and came from an important family in Japan. They were very compatible and had two girls. In 2000 they were 66 and at the peak of their careers. They had no intention to retire. They were excited about the twenty-first century and were excited about the future.

Sam and Jane Petrie would have been 85 in 2000. They had died in 1987. Sam had retired in 1980 at the age of 65. He didn't want to travel. He said, "My travels during World War II are enough." They retired to his ranch and looked forward to his grandchildren coming from Rochester to spend the summers with them. On November 12, 1997, he died in his sleep. His wife followed two months later. They were loved and missed.

Sergeant David Jones lived his life in Lamesa. He met yearly with his Army friends. His two boys took over the ranch. He retired in 1980 at the age of 72. He and his wife lived ten more years. He died in 1990 at the age of 82. His wife died six months later. Charles and Hideaki attended both funerals. They both felt that their generation was disappearing.

Akihiko and Ayame Okada were born in 1912. Akihiko had a remarkable career in academics and in business. They had two girls, and they married Japanese husbands. Their husbands were business men and worked in the family business. Akihiko retired in 1990 and enjoyed teaching at

Tokyo University. He became ill in 1995 and a few months later died at the age of 87.

When Akihiko retired, he came to Charles and told him how much he had meant to him over the years. He said, "I have always had trouble expressing love, but I want you to know I love you. Thank you for all of your kindness and caring." He hugged and kissed Charles on both cheeks. Charles felt it was a hello and a goodbye.

Ayame was barely alive in 2000. She was 88 years old. She would die on January 21, 2000. Their two girls and their husbands were active in the company family. They both had two children. Chie had two boys, and Chiase had a boy and a girl. All were very happy in 2000 and thanked their mother for the wonderful life she and Akihiko had given them. They were deeply saddened by her death.

Lillian's family did well with their 15 percent ownership of the Japanese real estate company. Dan and Lucy had all the money they needed and retired comfortably. They were able to help their children financially, and all were financially comfortable. In 1967 when they were driving home from Atlanta, they were struck head on by a drunken driver. They were killed instantly. The drunken driver had only a few scratches. Lillian was devastated as were all of the children.

In their Will the only asset that they had was with the Japanese real estate company. The children decided to sell it. They asked Charles to sell it for them. He advised against it, but they insisted. Charles bought it at a fair price, and they divided the money equally. Charles would now own 40% of the company. They had never really been a part of the company family. They refused to learn Japanese and didn't attend the company functions. They took a different road. The twenty-first century found them content in Athens, Georgia.

Now we come to Charles and Lillian. Charles was 75, and Lillian was 76 years old in 2000. They looked to others as being that age, but to them they were still the young lovers of 19 and 20. When Charles looked at Lillian, he saw that young beautiful blond headed, blue-eyed young lady that he fell in love with at first sight. At midnight when 2000 arrived, they were talking about their life together. They were asking each other, what were the important moments of their lives.

Charles was talking about his moments. He said, "Prior to the episode in the repo depo, I was a confused and frightened kid. When you came into the station and I saw the Japanese paratroopers charging and firing, I suddenly became another person. I stopped looking at life from the sidelines. I was suddenly a warrior fighting for my life and for a beautiful girl I had never met but admired from a distance. I was no longer confused or afraid, and I knew I could take care of myself. You surprised me that you were so interested in me when the fighting was over. I said to myself, 'If a beautiful girl could think I am okay, then I must really be somebody'. Lillian, your love and caring made me a man."

Lillian said, "Charles, I knew that men liked my looks, and I was flattered. I think I was a little narcissistic. But when I was lying on the floor of the aid station and bullets were flying every which way, and I saw you calmly fighting and forcing the Japanese to bypass us, I knew what I needed in life was a man, who would care for me and protect me. I looked at you carefully for the first time and saw how handsome you were, and I immediately told myself I had to capture you." They talked about the excitement of their first sexual experience. They reviewed all of the major events of their life together. They talked about all the crossroads they encountered. They centered on their cross road involving the events of 1980. Up to that time, Charles' activities were connected with business and medicine. The Vietnam War had intensified his anger about how their government was damaging its citizens' lives. He was 55 in 1980, and all he had done was just fume about the government's dishonesty and greed and it being influenced by money and power and not by the welfare of its citizens.

Lillian remembered that night when he suddenly announced he was going to run for the senator position from Minnesota. He told her he wanted an honest open government that trusted its citizens. That night they talked about how one gets elected to the Senate. Lillian said, "I feel that you start with people, who know you. You are known by nearly all of the physicians of this state. You have talked to all of their county medical societies. They see you as an honest and caring person. Go to them and tell them, what is troubling you. Tell them you feel that there is a need for someone in Washington DC that is interested in citizens having an open government -- a government that will represent the people's interest and not special interests. Indicate that you will not accept campaign money and will finance your expenses with your own funds. Ask all of them to help you get elected to the Senate. Ask them to use their influence with their patients in support of your candidacy. Keep your message simple." Charles was amazed at what Lillian had said. He said, "Lillian, I now appoint you my campaign manager." They did hire a professional political advisor to help. It took five years to accomplish this goal. He was elected for two terms. He joined the Senate at the same time his brother-in-law, Bill, was elected Senator from Georgia. They both fought for the same principles. They had some success. Lillian and he moved to Washington, D.C. and lived in a condo. They would go to Japan only in August when the Senate was not in session.

Towards the end of his second term, he told Lillian he was tired and he wanted to just be with her. They left Washington, D.C. in 1997 with no regrets. The next three years were fun times. They were like carefree kids. They spent many hours with their families. They looked at the clock. It was six a.m. They had talked all night. They went to bed and kissed good night saying the 20th century had been great, and now for the first time in a long time, there was peace. They expected that the 21st century would be a time of peace.

For you, who are reading this novel, must realize how wrong they were.

THE END

EPILOGUE

In 2010 we find all of the survivors alive and well. Hideaki is ninety-five and feeling like he can live another ten years. Aiko is struggling to keep up with Hideaki, but she is determined to live as long as he does.

Charles and Lillian are still traveling. They are in their mid-eighties and expect to live forever. They visit their children and their grandchildren. They spend more time in Japan than in the United States. Recently, Charles, Lillian, and Hideaki were awarded the highest civilian medal of Japan.

PRONUNCIATIONS OF JAPANESE GIVEN NAMES

Aiko -- ah ee' koh (Love Child)

Akemi -- Ah kee' mee (Bright Beauty)

Akihiko -- Ah kee hee' koh (Bright Prince)

Asami -- Ah sah' mee (Morning Beauty)

Ayame -- Ah yah' me (Iris Flower)

Chiase -- Chee ah' see (One Thousand Mornings)

Chie -- Chee (Wisdom)

Kazuki -- Kah zoo' kee (Harmonious Hope)

Hideaki -- Hi dee ah' kee (Shining Excellence)

Hideki -- Hi dee' kee (Splendid Opportunity)

ABOUT THE AUTHOR

Charles Samuel Betts lives in Little Rock, Arkansas. He is a retired psychiatrist. He has written genealogical books and this is his first novel. He travels with his wife to many countries. He is eighty-five years old and lives an active life. Like Hideaki he expects to live another ten years and then ask for more.

Breinigsville, PA USA
20 October 2010
247710BV00002B/83/P